MW00942803

ANGELICA'S LAST BREATH

Bestselling Author of *Fierce with Age*

ANGELICA'S LAST BREATH

Inspired by Leo Tolstoy's

The Death of Ivan Ilyich

Carol Orsborn

Introducing
the Fierce with Age Inspired Works Collection

Angelica's Last Breath is the first of three books that comprise Carol Orsborn's *Fierce with Age Inspired Works Collection*. Every one of the books included in this collection was inspired by the work of an author who has made a significant contribution to conscious aging over the course of the last 100-plus years.

Each book stands on its own, representing a different literary genre and phase in Carol Orsborn's late-life spiritual journey. Taken together, they are a beacon of light drawing inspiration from the past while illuminating the way forward for a new generation of elders who are becoming fierce with age.

THE COLLECTION

Angelica's Last Breath (Spring, 2018)

A novel inspired by Leo Tolstoy's The Death of Ivan Illyich

River Diary:
My Summer of Grace, Solitude
and 35 Geese (Summer, 2018)

A diary inspired by the writings of Thomas Merton

Older, Wiser, Fiercer:
One Woman's Meditation on the Measure
of Our Days (Fall, 2018)

Essays inspired by Florida Scott-Maxwell's The Measure of My Days

Inspired by Leo Tolstoy's *The Death of Ivan Ilyich* (1886); Bantam Books Version, Lynn Solotaroff translation (1981).

Cover photograph courtesy of Martin O'Connor Photography http://www.martinoconnorphoto.com/

This book is a work of fiction. Names, characters, places, and incidents are the product of the author's imagination or are used fictitiously. Any resemblance to actual events is unintended and entirely coincidental.

Copyright © 2018 Carol Orsborn, Ph.D.

www.Fiercewithage.com

All rights reserved.

ISBN: 1717102069
ISBN-13: 978-1717102065

To Leo Tolstoy

"Try to live with the part of your soul which

understands eternity, which is not afraid of

death. And that part of your soul is love."

—Leo Tolstoy

"When someone is on the point of leaving this world . . . the Shechinah shows herself to him, and then the soul goes out in joy and love to meet the Shechinah."

—Zohar III, 53a (Kabbalah)

Chest rising. The late afternoon air is as light as a bubble. A faint scent of incense, once so robust, lingers with the slightest trace of the many long days passed overlooking the ocean in tai chi practice—sandalwood/Chinese rain/burnt hay. Quelled now, by the presence of idle pain drips and empty oxygen canisters soon to be carted away. Antiseptic—on hands and bedrails, so recently abrasive, reads suddenly as refreshing mint, cleansing, purifying.

And the flowers! Bright red roses, newly arrived with a fragrance deemed too heavy for the room, briskly relegated to the back deck. The sliding glass door opens briefly to welcome a brace of salty ocean mist and slams shut again. Now only the scent of spring blossoms remains—sweet lilac, jolly daffodil and the steadfast joy of white jasmine. In the span of a single breath, a life— past, present and future—flashes by.

PART ONE

The Promontory

1

The last Saturday in April. Particularly chilly for spring, a season affectionately referred to by locals as "mud." Around the world, practitioners of tai chi gather on this day year after year in parks, fields, gymnasiums, and in the case of Portland, Maine on a promontory overlooking Casco Bay. The cool sun had melted most of the snow, and on this high ground, the flattened grass is thick and dry enough to provide firm footing.

Forty or so are gathered—teachers and students of various styles and schools, ages and levels of proficiency. A few onlookers rim the perimeter, where a handful of abandoned lobster shacks provide leaning posts and stumps. Backpacks and purses are scattered in informal piles, muffling the audible vibration of a missed phone call or text.

The honored teachers who have been selected this year to lead the group face the assemblage one by one, able in turn—if so inclined—to take note of the various sub-groupings: several affinity groups in a spectrum of colors that cuts across teacher, studio and style—pockets of deep pink, black and red. Proud competitors wearing distinctive sweatshirts reflecting personal allegiance and history.

The most poignant end of the spectrum centers around the deep pink—the studio colors of one whose absence is noted by all but the few who hang on at the outer fringe: Angelica Goodman Banks. In fact, it is a particular poignancy that if one knew where to look, Angelica and Charles Banks' back deck could be spotted below, one among a dozen townhomes, curved half-way around the broad circle of sand that clings to the edge of the ocean. It wouldn't take binoculars to notice the sliding glass door briefly open and slam shut, leaving a splash of bright red roses on the worn wooden railing.

Earlier in the day, in the first overly long transition between masters, two senior students who had started out at the same studio years ago took the opportunity to catch up. There was some small talk about how well Master Will's master classes were doing and had she heard that Angelica was ill?

"I'd heard she was in Quebec, on an extended writing sabbatical." The other shrugged.

So the day went, arms rising gracefully in unison like a flock of white cranes taking flight, feet advancing slowly in steps shaped like the letter C—right, left, right, left. After the final bow, most milled about, reluctant to leave. One went straight for his phone, eager to confirm a reservation for early dinner.

Instead, he let out an audible gasp which rippled through the gathering as others rushed to retrieve their phones and read the text that had been posted by the local newspaper for themselves.

Angelica Goodman Banks is dead. She passed away minutes ago after a lengthy illness. Breast cancer. At 51. Founder of the Angel Chi Style of Tai Chi, author of the bestselling book, 'Dancing with Angels: The Angel Chi Solution,' survived by her husband Charles Banks, a daughter Sophie and her sister Mira. Arrangements to be announced.

He who had initially sounded the alert with his sigh hurriedly resumed his retreat off the promontory lest his plans for dinner be derailed. He was followed, close behind, by two of the dozen or so of Angelica's students who had volunteered to represent their studio at the gathering. The two young women, dressed in the deep pink Angelica had chosen for her studio's color, were shocked. Less than two weeks ago, they'd been told that Angelica was doing well with her treatment, was using the time to write a sequel to her bestseller, and would be back to the studio by summer.

Elsewhere, lingering near the lobster shacks, small clusters of students clung together, quiet and somber. One of the locals ventured that she'd heard a rumor it had been stage four, metastasized. Another expressed regret that she hadn't made a bigger effort to visit—had heard it was only stage one, and that Angelica had been in remission. A woman closer to Angelica's age wept openly while a younger woman provided comfort.

The largest group milled about the elderly woman who had just led the final bow, long thin grey strands waving in the cold mist.

"What a tragedy."

"She was too young to die."

"I can't believe this happened—no warning."

"Did her daughter make it back in time?"

"Poor Charles."

All in all, the chill that swept through the dwindling crowd could be summed up in one thought: "If this could happen to Angelica, it could happen to me."

Who was this woman Angelica? a newcomer to the community wondered. She ventured forward to ask one of the honored teachers, a distinguished middle-aged man with thinning hair pulled back into a ponytail, dressed head to toe in a traditional red martial arts uniform, but he was already turning away from her in the direction of the even older Master Chen, robed, like many of the others, entirely in black.

"Will you go?" Master Will asked Master Chen.

"Ah, the funeral," Master Chen replied, rubbing his shaved bald head. "I doubt it. You?" But the question was rhetorical. Will sighed, considering too soon what Angelica's death would mean for his own prospects. With Angelica dead, and her only child

Sophie in China, there was no one with the necessary heft and charisma within her studio to carry forward her practice. *It was as good as promised to me*, Will Harman thought to himself. *A merger would be the way to go—I could easily move my students into her bigger space, wean her local followers off of Angelica's invented version of tai chi and back onto the traditional form. Throw in an occasional Angel Chi retreat for the out-of-towners.*

Will hurried home to tell his wife the news of Angelica's death. So much for her jealousy over Angelica's success, with her nagging that he spend less time aspiring for perfection of the form and more time growing his studio. At last he could satisfy both agendas. The thought refreshed his spirits as he opened the front door of his home.

2

Less than a mile from Will's home, the two students in dark pink who had hurried down the promontory were gently turned away at Angelica's townhouse door. There would be visitation for family, friends and students as soon as it could be arranged, the hospice nurse, an attractive, middle-aged Latina woman, offered. She left shortly thereafter, before the funeral transport team arrived, hoping to make it home before dark. On the way home, she'd pick up something special at the bakery—something with cinnamon and apple in it.

The three who had been closest to Angelica stood alone now, positioning themselves protectively around the bed. Having spent the bulk of his career in public relations, mentor and friend Martin Lyon knew how to keep his regrets mostly to himself, but despite his best efforts, the combination of guilt and grief showed plainly in his furrowed brow. Next to him stood Angelica's husband, Charles, his leading-man features blurred by a combination of too much beer, butter and unwanted emotion. Angelica's older sister Mira knew she should have been well-prepared for this death, having gone through the sudden passing of her beloved husband Morrie just three years ago, and the earlier deaths of their father and then, some decades later, her mother. But instead of getting good with death, she was more than ready to be finished with it.

Although it had not yet been an hour since the hospice nurse had closed Angelica's eyes, any signs of struggle had already dissipated. If only they hadn't been so immersed in the shock of their loss, they would have seen that the placid expression on Angelica's face was not resignation—but culmination.

3

Despite the pride they took in Angelica's success—including her public acknowledgment of her Jewish roots—the few traditional Jews who were part of the Portland tai chi and theater communities came early in a group, but left visitation quickly, surprised and disturbed by the open coffin.

"What next? Is she going to be cremated, too?" one asked.

"What do you expect when someone changes her name from Rena to Angelica?" said another. "At least they waited the three days."

"Is there any rabbi in Portland who even officiates cremations?"

Mira and Charles were, in fact, discussing this very thing in the funeral director's office at that moment, as the efficiently pleasant woman who had been assigned to them offered alternatives: a shaman in the Native American tradition, the interfaith chaplain from the local hospice, several ministers from New Thought spiritual centers and, of course, there was always the option of bringing in a freelance rabbi from Boston who the home had called upon in the past. Charles looked to Mira, having entered a state of deference in exchange for freedom from responsibility.

There was no hurry to return to the parlor, as she had already spent the most important part of the day—the early first hour before others arrived—alone at her sister's side. Her grief was acute but cold, more an expression of utter disappointment than love. Only distance and a practiced detachment had saved her from her anger at having been abandoned yet again. There would be no relief at the conclusion of this round of grief. Tears, meant to heal, were instead bitter and cold. Exhausted, she turned from the casket and headed to the private bathroom to clean up her tear-streaked makeup. If she had still wanted to be in touch with her thoughts, they would have been this: "Grief is a waste of time."

4

The salon was slowly filling with people. In the temporary absence of Mira, the two young women who had been turned away by the hospice nurse on Tai Chi Day, succeeded this time in assuming an official capacity. Dressed again in deep pink, they stood just inside the door of the salon, greeting the darkly-attired visitors as they entered. They knew nearly everyone who arrived: a number of other Angel Chi students including Allen, one of the few males who had followed Angelica when she'd left Master Chen's studio to start her own.

Standing at the open coffin was Ivan Dempster, the editor of the local newspaper who had been both the first in Portland to interview Angelica when her book first hit the *New York Times* bestseller list and again, more recently, about the *Angel Chi* sequel she was working on. In fact, it had been he who had posted the obituary notice just moments after Angelica passed, after receiving a text from one of the witnesses.

Now that he had arrived at his destination, he was confused—as many invariably are—about what was expected of him and, in point of fact, whether he should have come at all. The only thing he could summon up at the moment that seemed in any way appropriate was a prayer he'd learned in a Twelve-Step Program. He bent over the coffin in something of a bow, simultaneously using the opportunity to look about the room to see who else may have arrived.

Ivan recognized the middle-aged hospice nurse, Leticia Sanchez, who had previously attended the deaths of a number of people of note in Portland. Invariably, the wife or daughter would refer to the serenely plump woman, "Letty", as an angel who had graced the final hours with loving kindness. Standing nearby was Angelica's friend Sarah, the owner of the local bookstore, who was shivering helplessly in the presence of death. Joanne, a member of the board of the Chamber of Commerce, one of the bookstore's better customers, attempted unsuccessfully to comfort her. Finally, Ivan spotted the figure of the mayor brushing past the girls in pink. Making something of a bigger show of bowing, Ivan backed away at an angle, setting his trajectory in hopes they would casually intersect. He needed to fact-check one last bit of information for a story on a new commercial development, and this would save him the call.

There hadn't been time enough yet for most of the out-of-town visitors to make it to Portland—and what was true for Los Angeles,

Montreal and Milwaukee was nothing compared to Motuo, China, with its one avalanche-prone road in and out.

Among those the girls in pink did not know: three women and a man, seated around the perimeter, all middle-aged and groomed as if by the same barber and dressed in unfashionable dark suits by the same tailor. Each wore a cross and read silently from their well-worn Bibles.

As soon as Ivan vacated his spot coffin-side, Allen walked briskly across the salon in the same posture of apology he had adopted as the too tall and skinny teenager that Angelica had tried so hard to correct in over 10 years of classes. This was his first real death, given that even after all these years of training, he was still only 23. Sweetly, he had taken the time to write his master a long letter which he placed beside her on the deep pink satin pillow, careful not to disturb the perfect halo of salt and pepper curls that circled her head. Except for the shine and color of her hair, and the exaggerated thinness of her frame, she looked the same as when during the first of the Angel Chi retreats she'd guided him to meet his guardian angel years ago. As directed, he'd closed his eyes and visualized a figure emerging from shadows. At first, his angel had appeared to him as an Egyptian queen, large almond eyes circled darkly with black; brave, elongated nose and gold eagle's wings spread wide. But as she approached, the angel's ancient, bold features softened somewhat and in the end, she was simply Angelica.

Even in death she looked beautiful to him: relaxed, serene, complete. He had thought to stay longer, but as he gazed at Angelica, he felt increasingly unsettled. He had seen this expression before, on the handful of treasured occasions when he'd witnessed Angelica transcend teacher mode, losing herself in the deeply engrained movements that comprised the core of Angel

Chi. Under the present circumstances, it wasn't awe he was feeling—but shame. Angelica had died, and he was still here. Turning quickly from the coffin, he drew unwanted attention to himself as he bolted too fast for the door.

Celeste was relieved by the sudden departure, for she was now free to take her turn at the coffin and get out of there that much sooner. When all was said and done, standing at coffin's edge was not really all that different than the professional stance the town's top acupuncturist had adopted with the older woman all along, a neutral smile artfully masking her judgment that it had somehow all been deserved.

"So sad," she said to the two girls in pink, who held the door open for her as she exited. Celeste scanned the dozen or so arrivals who were milling about in the vestibule outside the salon. "So sad. So very sad" she uttered to all those she encountered en route to the front door.

"Hey!" a client responded too cheerily, having mistaken Celeste's pronouncement for a greeting.

Celeste found Master Will and Martin chatting on the front steps of the funeral home, where each had been startled by the speed of the opening door. Martin gave Celeste a quick hug and started inside but before Will could follow, Celeste grabbed his arm.

"Are we still on?" she asked.

"Go ahead. I won't be long," Will replied.

Martin took sour note of the brief exchange, only the boldness of the transaction transpiring as it did at the very portal of death holding any element of surprise.

True to his word, Master Will cut his visit short, nodding goodbye to Mira and Charles, who were walking slowly side by side back to the salon. Settled in his Prius, awaiting Siri's directions to the coffee shop, he took the moment to breathe in great gulps of relief while spontaneously offering up his deepest prayer.

"Thank God it wasn't me."

5

Unlike the funeral and the scattering of ashes earlier in the day, which had been limited to family, close friends and out of town guests, the reception was standing room only. The Angel Chi studio had been utilized a number of times for special events—its grand opening, of course, but also for Angelica's book launch and fundraisers for a variety of liberal and charitable causes. With its burnished dark bamboo wood floors, mirrored walls and the large picture window that opened onto the oyster bars on the quieter end of Commercial Street, the studio was at once impressive and welcoming. While Mira performed hostess duties with the same stoic professionalism she'd brought to the other funerals, something deep inside her was secretly coming undone.

This time, Master Will arrived on the earlier side, having swung by the acupuncture center to give Celeste a lift. In deference, he had installed a black suit jacket over his red uniform. Entering the studio, Will recalled how he and Angelica had walked the space together, deciding on which walls to place the mirrors, and the richest shade of pink for the paint. He'd had to walk a fine line, supporting Angelica after her split with Master Chen's studio where she'd received her training, all the while staying personally loyal to Master Chen—not an easy thing for him to have carried off in such a small town.

Spotting Will, Mira broke away from her son and his wife. The couple, who had started their long day's journey on a red eye from LAX, stood out primarily for being dressed inadequately for Portland's biting cool spring air. Will signaled to Charles, who was flanked by several elderly patrons of the theater company complaining loudly to him that the quality of acting had gone downhill since his departure. Nearby, waiting politely for their turn to express their sincere regrets, were three members of Charles' script-reading circle, each one more relieved than the next to no longer have to carry the secret burden of the true extent of Angelica's illness. Charles made his excuses, waved to his three friends, and headed toward Will and Mira, understanding that this was the moment he had been waiting for, the way out.

"You know Angelica thought the world of you," Mira reached out for Will's hand, and when he squeezed back, they were both touched. "Do you have a minute? There's something we need to ask you." Will turned to follow Charles and Mira to the private studio office, catching Celeste's encouraging wink. Celeste exhaled loudly and Mira was once more moved, taking this, too, as a sign of caring.

Of the three desks in the large brick office, Charles' had the best view out the large back window overlooking the harbor just above the garbage cans that lined the working portion of the waterfront alleyway. Angelica's desk faced the door, the late afternoon sun casting shadows on the vase and picture frame that had been left untouched. In the vase, a lone red rose had been allowed to wither and dry, several black petals resting on her favorite mousepad—a rubberized photo of Sophie, dressed in bright pink, doing the White Crane. A new full bottle of Sophie's favorite Jadore White Jasmine, given to her mother as a farewell gift, weighted down a stack of papers. (An opened bottle of the same expensive perfume, reluctantly relinquished by Sophie at the last minute when told the church wouldn't approve, now sat on Sophie's dresser just down the hall from Angelica's home studio.) There were several copies of Angelica's book strewn about. Mira had taken over the intern Jennifer's desk, which had been vacated ever since the girls' abrupt departure. Mira had quickly populated the empty in-basket with a neat but rapidly growing pile of files.

As discussed earlier with Charles, Mira had intended to get straight to the point with Will, motioning him to sit down. But with the door solidly closed behind her, words began tumbling out. Charles was aghast, watching his stoic sister-in-law unexpectedly unravel.

"You're so good to come, Will," she began. "Angelica spoke about you toward the end. Do you know? She stayed conscious through it all. I, we, felt so helpless, the pain, the suffering…" Despite her crisp posture, her voice started to crack.

"What about her hospice care?" Will offered. "They're usually so good with pain."

"Hospice. Yes. Our nurse Letty was an angel. But it was up to Angelica about the drugs, and she kept refusing, saying she could manage the pain. She moaned on and on and toward the end there were terrible screams. Charles was there. Oh Will, she was conscious through her very last breath." Her grief found the crack in her voice, a violent sob escaping her painfully tight throat. Charles rushed to put his arm around her shoulders, to comfort, but more to the point, to quiet her before the whole thing spun out of control. Will watched the scene helplessly, resenting the intrusion of the dreadful picture Mira had painted of her sister's agony and put off by Charles' transparent act of compassion.

Will remembered vividly the first time he saw Angelica. She was Rena then, Master Chen's senior student, grace and power in fluid movement. Some years later, during Master Chen's tragic absence, it was she and Will who had taken over the classes, generously supporting Master Chen as well as one another through a challenging time. Then, just two years later, her split with Chen tore a hole in the fabric of the tai chi community. But by then, she was well on her way to becoming Angelica—soon to be the owner of a new studio of her own, with a book in the works that was to make her a national celebrity. Of course, then there was the lawsuit that put a damper on her book's sales trajectory, that ugly business about Charles and the intern followed quickly by Sophie's unfortunate marriage. Indeed, the suffering had started well before the illness, Will noted. That the unbridled grief that had been loosed before him was about somebody that he not only respected and liked, but envied, and that the combination of emotions sparked the raw nerve of shame over the forced confrontation with his hypocrisy, would have taken him over had he allowed it to. But he was saved by the fact that before him, now struggling against her sobs was not Angelica, but Mira, the sister, someone he knew only superficially, and Charles, the husband, someone he knew well enough and didn't like.

In fact, it was because of Charles that he had avoided coming to the house after Angelica's diagnosis. He preferred to come and go directly to Angelica's studio for the master classes he'd been asked to lead in her place, stepping into the office only to collect his check. Will briefly considered leaving them to Mira's grief, but after a few moments, with both Mira and Charles apologizing profusely, and as taken aback by her outburst as were the others, Mira composed herself sufficiently to carry on. Despite the stain of the grief that lingered, they were all quietly relieved that Will had managed to keep an appropriate degree of emotional distance through the ordeal so that they were now able to get down to business.

"The studio," she said. "You know Charles has no interest in running it and Sophie's moved on. With Angelica's passing, we were hoping that…" Her voice trailed off, but she'd already said enough. Will was already thinking about how much bigger the Angel Chi studio was than his own space, and about all the improvements he could make. He also thought about the meeting at the coffee shop, the book Celeste had suggested they coauthor on the subject of what they would title *Power Chi*—not just mastering the meridians of our bodies and our lives in the service of personal healing and joy, as Angelica had done, but a muscular channeling of chi for the greater good of the entire universe. "Think big," Celeste had urged over dual cappuccinos, steaming in hand-thrown ceramic cups. "After all, if Angelica could do it, why not us?" Will had been intrigued, thinking how great the two of them would look together, seated side by side on the *Today*

Show. Will would do any of the demonstrating while his younger, attractive partner, also in red, would do most of the talking. That way he could simultaneously ensure the purity of the form while retaining a slice of the prized 18-34 female market.

"I know how hard this must be for both of you," Will reached across the desk for Mira's hand while sharing a hint of a sad smile with Charles. "If I can be of any help…"

Mira sighed deeply, pulling her hand away to pluck a manila folder from the top of the wire basket. Charles grabbed it from her and with a dramatic flourish, handed it to Will. Noting the enthusiasm with which Master Will accepted the folder, Charles now wished him gone as quickly as possible so that he could discuss some technicality about the dispensation of assets with Mira before the estate lawyer arrived.

PART TWO

On Stage

1

Just as her book stopped shy of the number one spot on the *New York Times* bestseller list, Angelica Goodman Banks, while exceptional, stalled just short of greatness.

She died at the age of fifty-one, the second daughter of Lillian, a self-taught bookkeeper for several of Milwaukee's independent bookstores, whose own mother was illiterate. Lillian was born in the gathering shadows leading up to World War II, a pretty but tough woman who thought of feelings as weakness, introspection as indulgence. "You think too much," she was fond of telling her daughter Rena, long before Rena changed her name to Angelica. Rena's earliest memory:

struggling to keep up with her mother at the department store, afraid she'd get left behind. Her happiest childhood memory: exiting the stage after her first starring role in a high school play, her mother, father and sister waiting for her backstage with a big bouquet of red roses.

Lillian and Ralph met at a temple sisterhood dance a few years after the end of the Korean War. Significantly older than Lillian, Ralph's career had outpaced most in his age group, thanks to an uneven gait which had excused him from the draft. Ralph Goodman had briefly aspired to become a doctor, but anxious to marry Lillian, he settled for a livelihood that he could launch in a matter of months not years. In short order he became a pharmacy technician, studying nights and weekends to ultimately become the kind of pharmacist who thought himself equal, if not superior, to the doctors whose orders he filled. His clients clung to his every word, as he answered their questions with a calm certainty that they often found more reassuring than the rushed directions issued by their own physicians. Rena loved her visits to the pharmacy, proud of her daddy's stiff white coat.

Back in her grandparents' Poland, a tight-knit community to be winnowed by pogrom, poverty and world war, it had been the norm for families to have eight or ten children. But born and raised in America, by the time the Goodman's started having children of their own, the family tree had but two sparse branches. Ralph's one brother became an academic and moved with his family to Canada where he landed a tenure-track position with a major university. The brother on Lillian's side was a gentle man, but slow. After showing up at a family event wearing his uniform from McDonald's, the Goodman's included his wife and offspring only when absolutely necessary.

Lillian and Ralph Goodman had just two children. Mira was "the sensible one." Bearing a striking resemblance to her mother, she had her pick of suitors. She fell in love with Morrie straight out of college because he was a happy man with good prospects: a middle-manager in a tool company that was performing beyond expectations. From the first, he took a big brother's interest in Rena's well-being. It was Morrie who at Mira's request made the dreadful call to Rena's dorm room in Madison to tell her that her father had been killed in a head-on collision. Rena was grateful and relieved that, when not long after Morrie landed a promotion to the tool company's west coast distribution center in L.A., they moved Lillian with them.

Mira sometimes wished she had the same spark that emanated from Rena. Her pull to be more like her younger sister never amounted to much, however, certainly not rising to anything akin to envy. Not that she wouldn't have liked to be their father's favorite. But the family had more or less informally split into teams, and she was her mother's pick. There was some kind of balance to their family life, not all to the good, but an acceptable enough balance of shadow and light that somehow worked well enough for the sisters. By the time she was a senior in high school, Rena had already carved out a persona unique to herself that she was to maintain the rest of her life: magnetic, deep-feeling and drawn to people, philosophies and spiritual systems that claimed access to higher truths. She could also be doggedly unaware of the difference between vanity and confidence. At Madison, she built on her success as an ingénue through exposure to acting methods and self-help books, digging beneath her characters' superficial layers to reveal deeper stratas of authentic motivation. Cast in a leading role first-time out, she was flattered by the director—with whom she'd had a brief affair. When she discovered that he had bedded several other students, she was as disgusted with herself as she had been angry with him. But later, when she moved to New York to start her acting career in earnest, she saw how readily those wielding power traded on pride and weakness. She could never bring herself to approve, but in time, she could recall even her abbreviated affair with a hard-won degree of equanimity.

When she landed her first role in an off-Broadway play, a walk-on in which she played a maid, she cashed in the last of her graduation savings bonds to buy a black turtleneck sweater, black designer jeans and triple-digit heels from a trendy East Village boutique. She took a room in an apartment with a rotating cast of aspiring actresses and models, one subway transfer from Times Square. Young and attractive, they blended in with an artsy crowd, sharing news of upcoming parties, auditions and gossip about temperamental artists, leading men and aspiring rock stars. Between jobs, she worked the register at an independent bookstore, with which her mother, although retired, had contacts. In her professional acting roles, she was determined to make a good impression, doing her homework for even the briefest of appearances.

Rena spent five years in this way before closing hard on 25. The very day she heard from a director that she was too old to be considered for the role of ingénue, she impulsively answered an ad in the theater trade classifieds. It was for the position of marketing director for a regional repertory theater company located in Portland, Maine. The classified caught her attention on multiple levels, not the least of which had been a seminal summer passed at an arts camp in the woods just north of town when she was 14. Her first time away from home, she turned out to be the only first-timer in a cabin of veterans. Like the wrong end of a magnet, Rena's natural charisma suddenly switched poles on her. She took refuge in judging the other girls as shallow and they thought of her as stuck-up. The summer was saved only by chance, when Rena encountered a hidden creek running through a mossy glade, cool and protected. Feeling something out of the ordinary all alone in the hidden recesses of the forest, Rena wrote her first poem. She described the underside of leaves, spider webs and the true nature of love. She snuck off to her creek at odd hours of the day, in the morning before breakfast, having done her cabin chores double-time. Mid-afternoon, with the script for the camp play under arm. And once, tip-toeing out of the cabin well after taps.

This was the night she encountered something bigger than poetry: something to which she could not put words with her eyes open. But with eyes closed, she could see what she was feeling as close to her as her own heart. An angel: not a Christmas card angel, gentle and cool with flowing blond hair, but an old woman, at least 50 years old, ringed by a halo of salt and pepper curls. And she had wings, at once ephemeral and shimmering—like dust illuminated in a beam of sunlight. Her slender body, robed in bright pink, glowed with an aura of unconditional love. Rena recoiled, but the angel held her fast, taking a single burning quill to emblazon her new true name on the young girl's forehead. As suddenly as the angel appeared, she departed, but not before having anointed the young girl with fresh courage. For the rest of the summer, she signed her new name, Angelica, to every poem. But at summers' end, she tore and tossed every page of poetry into the depths of the creek as some kind of promise but to whom or to what she could not articulate. Over time she forgot her poetry, her angel and her true name first for days, then months and finally years at a stretch.

When she landed the Portland job, Rena briefly considered turning it down, but one last failed audition convinced her that she should be grateful to have found a graceful way out. Her friends gathered together at a favorite bar in Williamsburg to wish her well. Before leaving, they posed for a photo of their farewell toast for which she bought a desk-top frame.

2

Portland, Maine is not New York City, not even Madison, Wisconsin for that matter. But it was in Portland that Rena discovered that she had the power not just to act, but to make things happen. She raised funds for the work of a new playwright and, on multiple occasions, delivered standing room only audiences. The position put her charisma, and her deep knowledge of human motivation, to practical, quantifiable use. She had a knack for entertaining donors and board members, one of whom took it upon himself to teach her how to wield her newly cultivated power to raise legacy-level funds and fill seats even for poorly reviewed shows. A marketer and promoter for an impressive roster of brand-name clients, the savvy board chair Martin Lyon showed Rena how to walk the fine line between influence and manipulation. On a professional level, he could be tough and demanding. But on a social level, especially with Rena after hours, he was sweet and attentive.

Rena was often seen on the arm of either Martin or the director, or in a theater pod including either or any of their casual boyfriends. On weekends between shows, she begged rides on friends' boats to explore inlets, islands and lighthouses. Under the setting sun, she pulled claws off of boiled lobsters, sucking out the sweet liquid that continued to flow after the hearty white meat had been thoroughly consumed. She vowed someday to live on one of the coves right on the ocean, and had every reason to believe that this was entirely within the realm of possibility.

It was 18 months from the time she arrived in Portland that she met Charles Banks. Like Rena, he had fled disappointing roles on Broadway for safe harbor. In Charles' case, given that some of the plays to his credit had gone on to win Tony's, he was pursued by regional theater companies throughout the northeast for leading roles.

Rena and Charles met at Martin's house at a fundraiser for big donors that Rena organized. Charles was, in fact, the draw, having been enticed to Portland from Broadway via a number of stops on the repertory circuit, with the promise of King Lear. The moment he entered Martin's Victorian home, Rena took charge of him. With her abundant head of dark curls, ethnic features and slender frame, she was not only attractive physically, but she carried herself with a fresh confidence that Charles found compelling. When she left to bring him a glass of champagne, Charles turned to Martin, who volunteered that Rena was the daughter he'd never had.

Even before they met, Rena had already deemed Charles Banks to be a suitable match, taking ownership of the advance copy of the biography his agent had sent over. Born on the North Shore of Lake Michigan, Charles got his start at Northwestern and then the Shubert Theater before heading for Broadway. He was known professionally as a generous actor on-stage and off whom, like his politically connected father, allowed his name to be used in conjunction with various liberal causes and campaigns. The bio revealed that he was ten years older than Rena, just as her father had been significantly older than Lillian. She would have preferred a younger man, but found the attention the leading man paid her flattering. In retrospect, years later, it occurred to her that his decision to stay on as the resident leading actor for the repertory theater was as much due to his exhaustion as it was to having found the love of his life. And, too, his generosity was revealed over time to reflect more a lack of boundaries and a tendency towards self-aggrandizement than altruism. But early on, with Charles having been offered the prize of a five-year contract and an option to renew, things progressed quickly for the lovers. Only Martin expressed his concern that she was rushing into things.

Rena Goodman and Charles Banks were married on-stage, Charles's mother flying in from Chicago. Mira and Morrie came out from L.A. with Lillian who made it known that the only reason she accepted this man as her son-in-law was because at her daughter's age, anything was better than nothing. The marriage ceremony was theatrical but brief, the party after blossoming into an inauguration for the new power couple. Shortly thereafter, they moved into the townhouse on Casco Bay. Furnished with modern Danish bought at the best store in town. A crate filled with the family's kosher china arrived from Los Angeles. With the job she landed at the *LA Weekly* blossoming to full-time on top of her parenting and caregiving duties, Mira preferred to serve on paper and Morrie went along with it. Charles found Rena's family's Jewish heritage to be interesting, but not intrusive. As long as they were free from any need to do anything about any religion, he was fine with it.

3

Another year passed pleasantly, with no reason to anticipate that anything could disrupt the cycle of fundraisers, rehearsals, opening nights, final bows and tear-downs they expected to enjoy together. But then something unplanned and to Charles's tastes, disagreeable, began to stir. Rena was pregnant. Theoretically, he was pleased with the notion of impending fatherhood. At 37, it was high time. And given his fans' warm reception to the news, he felt certain it only added to his brand. But on a day-to-day basis, he found Rena distracted and unavailable.

Rena was hurt by Charles' characterization of her desire to stay home rather than go out at night as "bad moods". She was relieved when he began finding reasons to attend cast parties and civic events without her, as they renegotiated their relationship invitation by invitation into something pleasant and workable but lacking the passion of the past. After the baby was born, they resumed their place at the best table of the latest hot spot or coolest café. Passersby, however, would now see an attractive mother fussing over the baby and Charles Banks slathering jam on croissants while bent over a script. His cappuccino was always dry, breve with an extra shot and double sugar while Rena sipped hot green tea.

Happily, the off-stage world of a theater company, with its kaleidoscope of interns, stage techs, and group ticket sales, proved to be an exceptionally amenable environment for Rena and Sophie. There was always a spare lap on which to bounce the curly-haired baby, and later, a collection of retired props that could easily be transformed into a creative playground for the growing child. Rena was happy enough with the arrangement, as long as nothing fell out of place to disturb the fragile peace. But Martin was among the few who cared enough to notice that the stress of managing husband, career and toddler was taking its toll. When an out-of-town critic gave Charles a harsh review, Rena, Sophie in tow, headed straight to Martin's office in the Victorian, downstairs from the very living room where she and Charles first met. In the front hallway, a traditional Buddha—thin, upright and austere—greeted clients and friends.

Charles had held Rena personally responsible for the review, she reported to Martin in measured tone. In truth, it was the worst fight they'd had. Still, Rena didn't want to draw too much attention to the incident, given that Martin still served on the theater company board. As he heard Rena out, he was struck with the thought that he should introduce her to tai chi—either to the newcomer to town, a martial arts prodigy Master Will, or to his old friend Master Chen, very much rooted in not only the old forms but the old ways. Will's studio, just getting started, had already won respect for faithfully adapting the traditional forms to a new generation's sensibilities, but he was young, still in his twenties. In either case, tai chi would help her with her stress and see things in larger perspective. He was about to say something about taking it up, but seeing the toddler Sophie clinging to her mother's scarf in one hand while grabbing at a shiny industry award on his desktop with her other, Martin realized that it would be years before Rena could fit something new into her life. Martin settled, instead, on loaning her his well-worn copy of *The I Ching*. It's about finding balance, he explained.

Four years passed before Martin introduced Rena to Master Chen. By then, Sophie was old enough to keep herself busy at the studio during the daily class. Rena told Sophie that they were "dancing with angels," succeeding at capturing her daughter's bright imagination. Sophie adored her mommy, and could often be found standing just off the polished wooden practice floor at the back of the studio, imitating the gentle movements of birds, snakes and dragons, or seated in a folding chair, coloring in books. Rena was glad she and her daughter had a place they enjoyed going together, especially during the long absences when Charles, invited to guest star with other companies in the region, found himself spending more time on-stage than off. Distance, interrupted by occasional amorous interludes, had become the normal state of affairs. However, this was less a problem to Rena, and more a solution.

She managed to spend less and less time with both her husband and her job, relying on the years she had invested in stockpiling her power at the theater company. She had a knack at picking her occasions wisely, be it showing up at an important meeting or procuring a key media placement for a show. Charles always got the benefit of her cachet to ensure, with the exception of the occasional renegade critic, the best interviews and reviews. Guest actors, however, were often managed rather than promoted, never knowing how it was that their chances had been spoiled. She quietly rejoiced in her level of life mastery, knowing that she had succeeded at wresting time and space to nurture her own and Sophie's vitality, and moreover, had done so without needing to unmask herself.

4

Increasingly, it was the tai chi, with its promise of self-mastery, that was becoming the organizing principle of her life. Martin had been right about that, introducing her to the thousand-year-old practice devoted to facilitating the movement of chi, a hidden energy visible only to fellow practitioners. Power for healing, for peace, for energy derived from the dynamic interplay of male and female, giving and receiving, activity and rest. In other words, balance.

From day one, she excelled. She practiced assiduously, on the back deck overlooking the ocean in the warm months, lighting incense and candles in the living room to practice indoors in the winter. Situating herself in the front row of the class, in a matter of months, Rena was Master Chen's pet. Her fellow students accepted her special status, some with admiration, and some with envy. Holding her arms in an embrace of chi, as if hugging a tree, she would stand sure-footed as Master Chen pushed on her shoulder to demonstrate how impossible she was to dislodge. Later at the townhome, before Charles came home, her daughter fresh from her bath would stand in the same pose, Rena's gentle push melting into a moist hug.

Sophie would be starting first grade soon. They had not yet decided on private or public, but given Maine's emphasis on quality education, both represented good choices. Charles had no opinion, but that was no different than any other decision related to their personal life, which suited Rena just fine.

PART THREE

The Alley

1

Rena Goodman Banks spent 13 years in this way, her home life distinguished primarily by her daughter's seamless progression through grades, and critical response to Charles' latest role. Rena's power with the company had continued to grow over time, only her succession of interns knowing how many of her wins were actually their doing. In the theater community, their complaints fell on deaf ears.

Martin knew how much of the work week Rena spent at Master Chen's studio, but since he was the one who had gotten her started, and because her results for the company were unimpeachable, he kept quiet. On a personal level, he was proud that Master Chen had given her a class of her own to lead: a beginner's lesson on Saturday mornings. On the rare occasion that Master Chen took ill, or had an unavoidable conflict, he asked Rena to take over the afternoon and evening advanced classes, and if Rena could not take them, he would ask a special favor of Will. Given that Will's classes at his own studio were so small, Will just brought his own students with him and referred to the intra-studio event as a "master class." Occasionally, Martin, who studied privately with Master Chen, would sit in to watch the group classes, marveling at Rena's grace.

What he didn't know—what nobody knew—is that Rena's description to her daughter a decade ago of tai chi as "dancing with the angels" was not just a story for an imaginative child. There were moments of practice, although few and far between, when thought stopped for Rena and heaven and earth fell into alignment. At the end of such a practice, sensitive enough to note the shift in energy, Master Chen closed the session with his sparingly offered praise "good class." But if he had known that it had been an angel that moved Rena, and not chi, he would have felt betrayed. Knowing this, Rena never mentioned her angel to anybody—except for Sophie, who despite her busy junior college schedule continued to come to classes whenever possible.

There was no reason to think that anything would ever disrupt the peace she had wrested out of life by the thoughtful application of power—to serve, to demand, to ignore and on rare occasion to transcend. Until late one night, walking alone in the harbor alley, Master Chen was mugged and beaten by a gang of teenage boys and left for dead. The unfortunate incident turned out to be the initiation of a chain of events that was destined to alter the course of Angelica's life.

The physical effects of the attack, from which he would fully recover, nevertheless forced Master Chen into prolonged absence. But the humiliation, that a martial arts master would have been brought down by a gang of children, left permanent marks.

In the months of Chen's recuperation, it was natural for Will and Rena to cover his classes and to discover that they enjoyed the comradery. As the weeks progressed, their conversations over hot green tea went deeper than teaching techniques, gossip about particular students and Master Chen's mental state. By the beginning of the second month, they were surfacing their respective philosophies about tai chi and life—Will taking the role of purist, Rena arguing for incorporation of Western symbolism into the Eastern tradition. Will advocated for a balance of male and female energy, the yin and the yang. Rena proposed that in a culture that was already privileged toward the male, it was an important and necessary corrective to restore true balance by giving female energies, like love, intuition and nurturing, more weight. In fact, in Master Chen's absence, she had become bolder—first internally, then finally, gingerly, testing her convictions with the students, stopping just shy of revealing her secret angel. By the time Chen returned, Rena's classes had grown to the largest numbers his studio had ever experienced.

At first, Rena's beginning students were excited to meet the real master. But they soon discovered that the rigid tai chi that Chen brought with him bore scant resemblance to what they'd been studying with Rena. In fact, during the months of his recovery, Chen had come to the conclusion that the source of his humiliation was that he had grown too soft, that the solution was to purge all that was not rooted in the tradition. All movements were now to be done in silence, no more Japanese flute music to set the mood nor incense to be burned. Eyes were open at all times, not closed; lights turned up bright, not dimmed. No hugging after practice, only formal bows directed to him. And Rena was welcome to join his classes but no longer invited to teach.

Rena took this as a lesson in acceptance, and vowed to submit humbly to Master Chen. And for weeks, he tested her patience, ignoring her while he demonstrated choke holds and elbow strikes, concentrating his attention on Allen and the few men in the class. That all ended the very first time he motioned her to the front.

"Punch hard." She complied. "Again." "Again." "Harder." "Again." "Again."

And on this last punch, he grabbed her arm, twisted it sharply, and she fell to the ground. She rose slowly, the class watching in silence. And it was in silence that she gathered her things and left the class, Master Chen shouting after her: "If you leave, don't come back."

"Master Chen!" the too tall-teenager, Allen, cried out.

"You, too. Get out." And not only Allen, but five others followed Rena out.

Her first thought was revenge, that she would start her own studio to punish that man for not only failing to appreciate her but for allowing his emotions to expose his weakness. It was all about his pitiful male ego, she told her friend Sarah, the owner of the biggest independent bookstore in town, the one woman in her circle of friends she could trust with her real thoughts. But that wasn't all. Rena had a higher-minded motivation to fuel her ambition. Rather than experiencing herself as banished, she believed herself to have been called to share her own special version of tai chi with the world, beginning with the loyal core of students who had followed her out Master Chen's door.

2

After a sleepless night, Martin chose to embrace Rena's split from Master Chen. In fact, seeing the promotional value in her new take on tai chi, he was the one who suggested she open her own studio and give her system a name. There were heated discussions between Martin and his old friend Master Chen, Chen warning that Rena was on dangerous ground, departing from the tradition on nobody's authority but her own. Martin and Chen went back far enough to trust that over time, he could smooth things over with his old friend at least on his own behalf, if not Rena's. Will attempted to stay out of it, but when Rena offered him $100 to rent out his small but adequate studio off-hours to incubate her system, his wife convinced him to take the money.

The local tai chi community split into variations of pro, anti and neutral to Rena's new system. Some praised Angelica's elevation of meditation and breathing techniques— some from the tradition, some her own—to front and center. Others criticized the addition of guided visualizations as "new age," dismissing the whole system as jerry-rigged. But none of that mattered as Angel Chi took off with a life of its own.

Rena found she could not tell the story about the split from Master Chen and the founding of her own form without making the part about the angel public, memorializing the creekside visitation that marked her initiation into mystical realms. In fact, the story became core first to the naming of her form, then to her studio, and finally to her book proposal, *Dancing with Angels: The Angel*

Chi Solution, and ultimately her conviction that the time had come to change her name from Rena to Angelica. When the newly-minted Angelica, with Sarah, Martin and her recently retained agent's help, sold her book idea to a major publisher for a large advance, her first move was to quit the theater company and move her studio from Will's space into a former restaurant that overlooked the very harbor alley where, ironically, Master Chen had been mugged. At Angelica's request, her daughter, Sophie, put her plans to transfer to UMaine in Bangor on hold for a year in order to help with the influx of new students, taking on classes for both beginning and intermediate students.

3

Charles was closing in on 60 when all of this was going on. When he first heard that Angelica was quitting the theater company, it was a betrayal. But shortly thereafter, in the middle of opening night of a newly commissioned work, Charles, in the leading role of a bombastic southern judge, had dropped the gavel. The gavel bounced noisily off the plywood desk and clattered stage right where the prop lay in plain view, while Charles was forced to thump the court to order with his barely audible fist for the remainder of the second act.

After twenty years of indulgence, in both buttered croissants and as a leading man,

Charles was ill-prepared to admit to the neuropathy in both hands and feet that had set in, before it was too late. While his contract precluded firing him for his advanced diabetes, he was no longer considered for leading roles. After a series of character parts, then walk-ons, he saw Angelica's enterprise as a way to save face. His decision to leave the theater company in order to manage her growing concern was neither entirely self-serving nor unwelcome. Both Charles and Angelica fostered the newly hatched hope that this new phase of their lives, transpiring beyond the shadow of his big career, held the promise of growing closer. Gradually, his resentment against the theater company, and her anger at Master Chen, subsided, and they were both sufficiently content.

Angelica was more cheerful and satisfied than she'd been in years as she split her time between working on the manuscript and teaching. She loved having Sophie around the studio, and Charles consistently went out of his way to tell Angelica how proud he was of her accomplishments and to bring Sophie a cappuccino breve dry to enjoy before class. Angelica was deeply immersed in her work, too busy for more than a quick hug, but feeling closer to Charles than she had in years.

4

Angelica embarked on her book tour, pleased that at the height of midlife, everything had worked out, the very synergy between internal and external that Angel Chi promised. Critics, interviewers and readers with an affinity for new thought praised the core principles upon which Angel Chi was based. First: There is an unseen order to the universe. Second: Our highest good lies in harmoniously adjusting ourselves to this unseen order. Third: Whatever keeps us from experiencing our alignment with the universe is accidental. Fourth: By calling upon the power of one's personal angel, any impediment to mastery of these principles can be overcome.

Advance sales merited touring to 8 cities, but by the time pub date approached, Martin, in conjunction with the publisher's marketing staff, added on just shy of three more weeks of dates to climax with a major co-promotion with Amazon. She left the studio to Sophie, Will and Charles and the new intern Jennifer, to be assisted by Allen, and concentrated on completing the transformation from Rena to Angelica on a national scale. She studied the clothing styles of both authors and spiritual leaders, imagining the ideal to which she aspired. White for Angelica would be too obvious, gossamer too trite. She fell asleep at night mixing and matching designer scarves with soft jackets culled from Nordstrom online; Mao style jackets in red silk; black cashmere with a single strand of pearls. When she settled on deeply textured pullover knits in royal blue and emerald green, softly pleated black pants, oversized earrings and the highest possible heels, she was thrilled.

Just prior to leaving on tour, she'd gathered the family and staff, including Martin, Will, Allen, her good friend Sarah, the intern Jennifer and her acupuncturist Celeste, to surprise them with her new look. She looked amazing, they all agreed, toasting her with a round of champagne. In the weeks to come, there would be non-stop interviews, book signings and on-air demonstrations of Angel Chi.

Atlanta was the first stop on her tour. At the airport, her driver, on retainer with the publisher, recognized her immediately by the originality of her carefully crafted look. Angelica's book sales numbers were strong, so she was put into the best hotels with bouquets of flowers and bowls of fruit, although she was to be in the room only a few hours between her last late-night interview and the first of the morning shows. Feeling charmed, she considered it but a small misstep when the book editor at the *Denver Post* neglected to mention that this interview would be more than talk. The writer, who had taken tai chi at the Y, asked Angelica to show her the moves. Caught up in the moment, Angelica neglected to kick off her Jimmy Choos, one of which snagged in a tear in the industrial carpeting. Angelica fell forward, bumping her chest on the corner of the journalist's desk, but being a master at balance, was proud she caught herself before falling all the way down. The bump raised a large bruise on her left breast, but the pain quickly subsided, going from acute to dull. The article mentioned the incident in complimentary terms, commending her graceful recovery, and gave the book a wonderful review.

Waiting for the flight to Los Angeles, she emailed the story about the bump to Sophie, Charles and Martin. "Proof my system works. All I have to show for it is a bruise and a bunch of book sales." To which she received a smiley face (Sophie) and an "atta girl"

(Martin.) Nothing from Charles, but he'd become quieter and quieter over the course of the three weeks she'd been gone.

On the whole, things were progressing to her satisfaction—her only frustration that it was taking longer than she'd hoped to rise to the top of the best seller list—stuck first at number 10, then number 5—but rising it was. The publisher assured her that with the big Amazon promotion they had scheduled, it was only a matter of time before she hit the number one spot. It was in Los Angeles, the last stop of her west coast swing, and during a congratulatory if hurried lunch with Mira between interviews, that she got the news that the *New York Times* had agreed to an interview. Ebullient, she not only repeated the story about her attempt to perform her signature move in heels, she jumped out of her chair to demonstrate it. The bump, she confessed, was still tender to the touch—but nothing like it had been before.

5

Although Angelica left LAX at a reasonable hour, it was early morning before she checked into the W in Manhattan. She hoped to get at least a few hours sleep before the big interview, but the message the night clerk handed her was to change not only that, but everything.

"NYT postponed. Coming in from Boston. Meet me at Union Station Oyster Bar at noon. Will explain everything." Signed by her agent, Barrie Moss.

Barrie was one of Martin's first employees, having made the switch from publicist to book agent at the same time she'd come out to friends and family and moved from

Portland to Boston. Angelica had met her agent in person only twice, the day she signed the contract with her in Portland and the day she signed the contract with the publisher in Manhattan.

Barrie had hastily thrown a designer maroon cocoon coat over jeans in order to make the first Acela, installing herself in a quiet corner of the dark, noisy restaurant. She attempted a smile but Angelica's anxiety was not abated. Something was wrong. Barrie got right to the point. A lawsuit had been filed and an injunction granted. With her book sales soaring, the publisher had hoped to spare her news of the suit—that kind of thing dogs authors on the bestseller list all the time. But the injunction was something they had to take seriously.

"Lawsuit? For what?"

"A reader, a middle-aged woman in Des Moines, followed your instructions on page 65—the Angel Chi Healing Breath exercise.

She passed out, hit her head on the floor and ended up in the hospital with a concussion. She's suing you and the publisher for damages—in the millions. Angelica, I have to ask you. Where did you get that exercise? Is it from the tradition, or did you make it up?"

"Make it up? What difference does it make? Because some random woman in Indiana…"

"Iowa"

"Faints and blames it on me, the publisher cancels the *New York Times* interview?"

"Look, be glad they're not pulling books already in the pipeline. But no more promotion—and no second printings—until they add a disclaimer. Everybody believes this will blow over. After all, your book is making a lot of money for everybody. Just think of it as a nuisance."

That so-called nuisance signaled the end of Angelica's book tour, terminated abruptly five days early. In a conciliatory gesture, Barrie offered to gather up Angelica's luggage from the W and have it delivered directly to her in Portland so that Angelica could make the 2 o'clock Acela home.

Allen was first shocked, then delighted, then shocked again to see Angelica at the studio door. The slow-moving rows of students in the advanced class froze in form as the two hugged awkwardly before heading for the office. Where was Sophie? This was supposed to be her class.

Before either could say anything, Angelica surveyed the scene. Her desk had remained untouched, the vase with a single rose sadly wilted, the framed Williamsburg picture, a stack of her books. Sophie's messy desk was covered with files, Charles's desk was bare with the exception of a pile of film scripts and the intern's desk had been hastily cleared off, crumpled papers and Kleenex blotted with lipstick scattered around the base of the trash can.

"Where is everybody?" Angelica asked.

"We weren't expecting you back until next week." Allen knew this was a woefully inadequate answer, but it was all he had in him.

"Sophie—is she okay?"

"She's fine. They're all fine." He grabbed into his pocket. "Here's where you can find Sophie. She said it was for emergencies."

It was the address for a Baptist church on the north side of town.

6

Even though it was evening, the Third Baptist Church was full of people, lights blazing and a gospel choir booming. The church receptionist knew immediately where Sophie was to be found, retrieving her from Bible Study.

Sophie loved her mother—they'd always been close, maybe too close—but she knew that this encounter was taking them both onto uncharted territory and it showed in her eyes.

"Sophie, are you okay? What are you doing here? What about your class?"

"You're back early. What's wrong?"

"That can wait. You first."

Sophie hesitated, then seeing her confused mother's concern, caved.

"I met someone."

"You met someone?"

"Mom, let's not do this here. I'll meet you at home when I'm through. I'll tell you everything."

That night, Sophie told Angelica that she'd met Justin Taylor a few weeks ago, waiting in line at Starbucks. Tall, handsome, with a winning smile and kind eyes... a missionary, back to his home church in Portland between assignments.

"You always said you wanted me to be happy" she responded to Angelica's wordless protest. "There's nothing wrong with dating a Christian. You married a Christian. It's okay for you but not for me?"

"Dad's no Christian. He's nothing," Angelica blurted.

"I'll say," Sophie muttered under her breath.

"Sophie. What's going on?"

"I'm not going to cover for dad any more. As soon as you left he went AWOL. I've been stuck at the studio doing all his work plus teaching my classes, while you're running around the country leaving me to deal, and I'm done with all of it."

And so Sophie was. Within a month, and despite a series of heated arguments with her mother and father, Sophie was baptized; within eight weeks she and Justin were married at the church, Angelica and Charles reluctantly agreeing to walk her down the aisle. By April, admittedly rushed in order to beat the rainy season on mainland China, and accompanied by a great deal of tears, Sophie and Justin were given a two-year posting to isolated and remote Motuo, located in the mountainous Autonomous Region of Tibet.

Angelica cried out to Sophie when she heard the news of their assignment. Justin and Sophie, in the company of his parents and several church leaders, explained the nature of their posting, attempting to put what they recognized was a blow to Angelica into larger context.

"Until now, the only way in was a dangerous route navigated by foot over frozen terrain and a perilous 600 meter long suspension bridge, impossible for the missionaries to navigate," Justin offered while Sophie nodded in support. As it turns out, just as their marriage was consummating, a long-awaited road and upgraded bridge, delayed multiple times by avalanches and mud slides, had been declared passable. The young couple had taken this to be a sign that they were being called to bring the Good News to the unfortunates of Motuo and offered themselves up.

7

That left Angelica and Charles. It soon became obvious that Charles had, indeed, neglected to keep up management of the studio during her book tour. He had also taken the opportunity of Angelica's absence to take a brief fling at a midlife sabbatical— determining to begin a new, if ultimately short-lived career, as a screenwriter. In this, he had been encouraged on multiple levels by the pretty young intern, Jennifer, who happened to be the best friend of Angelica's acupuncturist, Celeste. After a few long weekends of Charles off "on a writing retreat," during which the intern had also gone missing, Sophie confronted her father, stormed out of the studio and headed to Starbucks.

By the time Angelica's book tour ended, as premature a return home as it turned out to be, the intern was already over and gone. Charles determined to pretend that none of this had happened. In the tumult around Sophie's conversion, engagement and the lawsuit, Angelica took her inspiration from both the *I Ching* and Martin, who advised her "to let many things pass without being duped."

While the town buzzed about Charles and Jennifer, the closest Angelica ever let on to admitting to the affair was to stop going to acupuncture with Celeste and take up Reiki instead with a gay masseuse, one of Martin's friends. As for the lawsuit, as her agent had promised, it amounted to nothing when a witness came forward saying she had seen the woman fall on black ice and hit her head while walking her dog. The publisher's insurance covered all of Angelica's legal fees, the Fed Ex packets containing legal documents finally stopped coming, and all that remained was the book's slippage from the heady Number 5 on the bestseller list to 20, 30 and finally 50, where it hovered long enough to make everybody but Angelica sufficiently happy.

It was all too much, and Angelica spent more than one sleepless night telling her angel off. Every morning, over her green tea and his latte, she ran her litany of complaints past Charles, mistaking the look of daily relief that he and Jennifer had not made it onto her list as encouragement. In fact, he was equally relieved to have a good excuse to leave his brief fling with both the girl and screenwriting behind, having proven to himself that he had neither the energy nor talent to master either at his age.

Angelica recognized Charles' relief, enshrouded by the simple pleasure of their morning ritual, and decided in an instant that it was not too late, after all, for either of them. She would redouble her commitment to the studio and to their marriage and make the most of what remained of her residue of celebrityhood. As Angelica's studio emerged from the shadow of the lawsuit, Charles once again picked up the reins of day-to-day management, grateful to have gotten off so easy.

8

Things soon returned to what Angelica thought of as "the new normal." They continued their morning ritual, Charles taking his coffee black in a renewed effort to watch his diet. They drove together to the studio and, when Angelica wasn't teaching, sat side by side at their respective desks. There was a steady stream of students in and out of their office, some heading to Charles to work out payment plans and to schedule make-up classes. But most were there for Angelica, not only asking for advice about Angel Chi, but all manner of personal concerns. Their response to her guidance ranged from appreciation to adoration and she prided herself on having hard-won wisdom to share. But after the black ice incident, she was careful to have all her students sign disclaimers. Too, there were those in the greater tai chi community who spoke against her, albeit gratified by her sinking rank on the bestseller list. She met the occasional report of such gossip or judgment with a casually practiced dismissive shrug that her followers took as saintly.

With Sophie gone, Angelica realized just how much her daughter had been covering for Charles. His math was sloppy, so when he stepped out of the office for lunch with a friend, she would quietly go through the books and make corrections. Where Charles made his greatest contribution was in hosting and attending the occasional event, the studio loaned out to various charitable causes around town. His gift was not in event logistics, which were handily delegated to junior members of Martin's staff. But in having retained enough cachet with a certain class of patrons to ensure that despite the gossip, Charles and Angelica Banks continued to attract A-list attendees from the greater Portland area to the events they hosted, as well as invitations to the best parties in town.

Mostly there was a negotiated peace between them, but they did argue from time to time. Usually, the fights were over trivial matters. At one important social event they'd hosted at the studio, Charles had neglected to tell the caterer to make everything gluten free. Squaring off in their office, door shut, she blamed him and he blamed Martin's staff. Angelica whispered in as loud a venom as she dared, calling him good-for-nothing, always shifting the blame to others. He responded in matched volume and tone by calling her a control freak and a shrew, always thinking she was superior to others. But when Martin knocked on the door to tell them that a particularly important guest had arrived, they took up hosting duties seamlessly, and none of what had transpired showed to the guests.

Angelica missed Sophie terribly, but had finally managed to bury her fear that her daughter spoke the truth when she essentially called her a fraud and a hypocrite, an accusation that cut much deeper than the question of interfaith marriage. She derived great pleasure from the occasional interview opportunities that continued to come in, and the requests for information about upcoming Angel Chi Retreats from Facebook followers from around the world. They held the special retreats at the studio about once a month, ranging from one to five days. For the longer retreats, she called on Will to help out, and he always said yes. She never gloated in either the flattery she received, or in her daily replenished conviction that she was, indeed, specially chosen to do God's work.

Over the days, weeks and months, Charles and Angelica added new and higher quality people into their circle of friends, not just the cream of Portland society, but internationally known authors and healers passing through Portland on media tour or holiday. An heiress from Boston travelled by limousine to Portland in order to issue an invitation to Angelica in person. She offered her the opportunity to travel together through India and Asia during which she would introduce Angelica to her personal friends, the Dalai Lama, Gurumayi and Sri Sri Ravi Shankar ji. Of course, Angelica would be her guest, but Angelica, reluctant to leave Charles to his own devices again, demurred.

So things went, balance and stability established and everything under control.

PART FOUR

The Waiting Room

1

Charles' diabetes was being sufficiently well managed. While the neuropathy was irreversible, they had caught it in time before even more unpleasant symptoms manifested. Angelica, too, was in good health, but for a bitter taste in her mouth that could not be assuaged by mouthwash or organic toothpaste. She stopped eating dairy, which she hoped would solve the problem. But then, too, there were what she thought of as "episodes." Leading a class, or even practicing her Angel Chi form alone on the back deck, she began experiencing micro-phase-outs. These momentary interruptions in her energy flow passed through so quickly nobody but she knew that one had occurred. Web MD identified her symptom as anxiety spells, so the only one she spoke to about her episodes was her new Reiki practitioner, Philip, Martin's good friend. Philip always dressed in white from head to toe and preferred to be called Flip. Flip passed his hands over her energy field and assured her that he could not sense any gaps or interference, but that her life force, overall, was weak. Upon his urging, she went to bed earlier and spent more time in silent meditation, but to no avail.

There was a third issue, the one that worried her most. Every time she was alone, her fingers compulsively returned to the spot on her breast where the bruise had now faded entirely. Over and over again, she searched, discovered and dismissed an unevenness of texture, sometimes perceived as a thickening, sometimes as nothing. But none of this added up to much, and could hardly be considered to mean she was ill.

Despite trying several new brands of mouthwash, the sense that something was off refused to abate. Angelica had already been through a lot, relying upon her Angel Chi practice to transform the shocks that had come her way into personal growth. But gradually, even something as simple as having to stand too long in the grocery store line or being put on hold by her agent grew from merely irritating to undermining.

Eventually, her peevishness spilled over, the more perceptive in her inner Angel Chi circle noticing that something was not quite right. Given their respect for Angelica, each took it, rather, as a sign of some shortcoming on his or her own part, vowing to make a bigger effort to get to class on time or volunteering to help with the newcomers before practice.

Charles was not so inclined to take her bad moods upon him, complaining to his old theater friends over his two beer limit that

Angelica had become impossible. With a select few, he defended his short-lived tryst as having been inevitable, justified even, given Angelica's life-long love affair with herself. In fact, he argued that she had always been selfish and controlling, and that only someone with his generous and patient character would have lasted this long with her. The two quarreled frequently, and it was true that Angelica was more often than not the instigator. After a month of skirmishes over whether the electricity bill had been paid on time and why the upcoming Angel Chi Retreat had unsold registrations, Charles and Angelica began avoiding each other when possible.

2

The Angel Chi Retreat sold out, but in the haste to fill spots, an angry fundamentalist—known to rail against tourists along the cruise line dock—had inadvertently been permitted to enroll. His presence was revealed when early on during the retreat he was asked by Angelica to close his eyes and visualize his guardian angel emerging from shadows. The young man suddenly began screaming.

"Be gone Satan, fallen angel Lucifer. Jesus Christ, save us sinners from the wrath of God. Confess your sins to Jesus, witch, and ask Him to cover your sins with His blood."

Shaken but in control, Angelica called a break and Allen helped her escort the disturbed young man to her office where she had expected Charles to calm the situation, issue a refund check, and show the young man out. Charles, however, was nowhere to be found. Moreover, the checkbook was not on its accustomed shelf, so she was forced to not only dig into her own purse scrambling for $20 bills, but borrow from Allen.

By the time Angelica and Charles faced off at dinner, he stood accused of not only being in league with the devil, himself, but responsible for Sophie's bolt to China. When this harsh assertion was met by silence rather than retort, Angelica recognized that she had gone too far. If she had not then unconsciously brought her hand up to her breast, Charles may have stalked off. Indeed, in the silence, a wave of hatred swept through him, and for a moment, he wished her dead. But of course, it was Angelica who was now paying the bills. He resented needing her, but his exasperation surfaced uncharacteristic insight. Something was wrong with her, something about her breast.

"You've got to see your doctor," he issued with as little venom as possible, and surprising them both, Angelica agreed. She called Dr. Edmund Clark the next day.

3

When asked if it were an emergency, she replied no, so the appointment was made for the following week. She'd been to see Dr. Edmund Clark every year for the past fifteen years, a routine affair that shrouded otherwise intolerable intimacies in institutionalized ritual. She never demanded more of him, having pulled strings to join his practice after the kindly physician who attended the birth of Sophie retired. But Angelica had already broken protocol by arriving six months before her annual exam to the celebrated doctor's busy waiting room and its padded chairs filled with young women glowing in various stages of pregnancy.

Everything was just as she'd expected: the too-long wait outside and then again inside the examining room as she balanced in a flimsy paper gown on the cold metal table. There was the perfunctory greeting and familiar cold fingers kneading her breasts as a bored nurse stood guard. Every word and action exuded an aura of solicitous importance as Dr. Clark consulted Angelica's chart and studied six darkly illuminated films of her breasts, hung neatly side by side. His few pointed questions demanded prompt responses while hers were met with a wry smile that implied: "I'm in charge here. Nothing you say or do will change the outcome so please don't waste your breath." It was the same smile she, herself, had assumed when encountering one or the other of Master Chen's students who after all these years persisted in asking when she was coming back.

"Fibrotic breasts", the doctor announced. "Fibroids."

Dr. Clark expected this to be sufficient, having previously dismissed her episodes as anxiety spells, the bitter taste as acid reflux and giving her a prescription for a mild tranquillizer and Omeprazole. "Any questions, follow-up with your internist."

All Angelica wanted to know was whether it was something to worry about—or not. The doctor did not address her question directly, instead turning to the x-rays and rambling on a bit about random calcium deposits that had showed up some years ago and that had remained unchanged. Taking off his black rim glasses, Dr. Clark finally turned back to Angelica, educating her about the complexities of age-related changes, entirely normal; lumpy breasts and calcified milk ducts and so on, once again, briefly considering alternative explanations of each symptom then dismissing the lot of them as inconsequential. "Of course, the shadow on your mammogram will continue to be watched. If it were to grow, we would have to reconsider the diagnosis and in that case, it could indeed be something serious." There was a too long moment of silence. "Take a note," Dr. Clark turned to his nurse. "Move her mammogram up three months."

The note in her chart sealed her fear. This was not all in her mind, but rather a tangible shadow on a dark film that merited watching. The shock of it, part self-pity, part resentment, swept through her. But she said nothing, waiting her turn in line at the scheduling desk to reset her annual mammogram for three months early. Out of the corner of her eye, she glimpsed the doctor enter an examination room, undoubtedly about to affirm the presence of new life or the position of a fetal head.

She left quickly, embarrassed by the visible shadow she was certain trailed behind, apparent and abhorrent to every pregnant eye.

4

Angelica went home the long way. Starting out at the medical center parking lot, driving past the town's history museum housed in an old church, then rounding the corner to her studio, she ran and re-ran every word, seeking anything she could use to make sense of the one question that remained: "How serious is it?" She could see through the picture window that opened onto Main Street that the studio was empty, lights off, and to her shadowed vision, it not only looked empty but abandoned. *But why if it is just a calcium deposit is it being watched? If it had been on my films for years, how is it that it hadn't been brought to my attention as a cause for concern earlier?*

Driving on, through downtown, along the harbor, over the bridge in the direction of her townhome, everything she saw appeared dismal, the tourists rushing back onto the cruise liners for an evening departure, the dilapidated lobster shacks and wind-battered piers. She pulled into her driveway, sidling next to Charles' car, an older model BMW, and sat. *Could it be serious? How serious? Or is it truly nothing to worry about?* Her hand responded instinctively, going once again to its familiar place on her breast—tracing the outlines of what had suddenly seemed to have coalesced into a lump.

Charles put down the script he was, unbeknownst to Angelica, considering directing somewhere. He listened to her account one time through, but when she started over again, he interrupted her more abruptly than intended.

"What a relief," he said. "I'm so glad you went to the doctor. I'm heading into town and can pick up the prescription for you." Angelica ignored the interruption picking up at the exact place toward which she'd been heading.

"What do we tell Sophie?" Angelica called after Charles as he sprinted for the door. In the four months since her departure to China, there had only been two letters from Sophie, all loving and full of good news. But the church had forewarned them that communications to and from Motuo were spotty, at best. If it weren't the rainy or winter seasons with their mudslides and avalanches rendering the already difficult road impassable, and if it were a true emergency, there was a Himalayan courier the church could call upon, but at great expense. Even so, it could take weeks to get a message through.

"Heartburn," said Charles. "That's what we tell Sophie. Exactly what the doctor said.

Heartburn." Charles was gone, and Angelica took her first deep breath in hours.

Charles was right. How silly it would be to dispatch the Himalayan courier for a case of acid reflux. Maybe it's not so serious after all.

5

Angelica took the heartburn medicine as directed, passed on the tranquillizers, and went online to research recommended changes in her diet. No more tomatoes or caffeine, not even her favorite green tea. At first, the sacrificial acts brought her some comfort. But when the bitter taste in her mouth and the episodes persisted, Dr. Clark's office responded with a referral to a gastro-intestinal specialist who wanted to stick a tube down her throat. What did her esophagus have to do with the lump growing beneath her worried fingers? When she tried to get this question directly to Dr. Clark, she received a call back from the nurse: "Dr. Clark says to follow up with the GI specialist, and that he'll be happy to answer any questions you might have at your next scheduled mammogram."

By defying both the endoscopy and tranquillizers, Angelica feared that any further outreach would brand her a "troublemaker." She fought the urge to call her sister, Mira, in L.A., anticipating that the empathy she would be tendered would come coupled with bossy advice. In any case, she was not ready to go public with her concerns, and in its place developed a sudden, voracious appetite for stories—both online and off—about symptoms that even vaguely resembled her own. Feigning mere curiosity, Angelica brazenly broke into conversations overheard at the dry cleaners and grocery store, engaging with complete strangers about illness, symptoms and prognosis.

Meanwhile, she took her medicine and watched her diet, convincing herself that she was getting better. This strategy worked as long as nothing went awry with her life. When Charles got his math right and the retreats sold out, she felt reassured that nothing was truly wrong. But with the smallest misstep, her hand flew to her chest and she remembered the serious implications of her situation. Normally, she could absorb life's blows with admirable graciousness. But now, she found herself ricocheting between rage at her doctors, irritation with Charles, despair over the unfairness of life and the worry that she had somehow brought this upon herself.

Angelica had sufficient self-awareness to recognize the toxicity of her negative thoughts, which only made matters worse. What she needed now—what she had trained for over the decades—was peace: body, mind and spirit working together in unity. Her Angel Chi breathing techniques left her light-headed, but just as troubled as before. Her angel had resisted her most urgent summons.

The taste in Angelica's mouth became more stringent, the phase-outs longer and the changing nature of the breast beneath her fingers more insistent. Moreover, what began as a health-giving diet made her weak and she soon took to taking naps every afternoon that failed to refresh. She responded by doubling up her efforts to take matters in hand. No more self-pity. Only loving thoughts. Step up her Angel Chi practice, not just in the studio while leading the class, but alone in her townhome living room, incense glowing in the twilight. She also increased her Reiki sessions to two times a week and paid a visit to the homeopath Flip had told her about.

The homeopath diagnosed the bitter taste as well as all of her other worries as the effect of too little rather than too much acid. She assured Angelica that all would be well, and sold her six bottles of herbs and tinctures to take home with her. These Angelica swallowed in the privacy of the bathroom down the hall, not feeling up to a discussion about it with Charles. When after a week nothing had improved, she dumped the bottles in the trash. But before going back to her heartburn prescription, she briefly considered consulting a healer her hairdresser told her about, a chiropractor who used gems and crystals to cure everything from headaches to cancer. Amethysts and selenite among them, a prescription of healing minerals to be laid in a grid across her chest during the session and taken home with her to be arranged in a similar geometric pattern around the base of the lamp next to her bed.

Stones…for something as serious as this? Appalled at her own desperation, she vowed to stop floundering, and do just as Dr. Clark ordered before she had started second-guessing him. She returned to a normal diet, resumed her medicine and resolved to wait with renewed patience for her mammogram.

6

Her resolve was sincere, but proved to falter at the slightest provocation. She continued on at the studio, but there was no fooling herself. Something was lurking in her of such magnitude that nothing that had come before could ever compare. And in this, she was all alone. Whether Allen and her core students chose to ignore the seriousness of her situation—or truly were unaware—Angelica resented the customary busyness that continued unabated about her. Classes began on time, green tea was poured from the communal pot, the next big retreat was scheduled with Will invited to help teach the basics to first-timers in the back of the studio.

Charles continued to be irritated with Angelica for holding it together at the studio then sulking at home. He rarely said it out loud, but he was now convinced it was all in her head and that this so-called illness was just another way of making his life miserable.

At the retreat, Angelica glimpsed, or thought she did, Will eyeing her from the back, as if her spot up front were already vacant. Surrounded by devoted students at the end of the retreat, she suffered one of her episodes. The incident escaped notice but rendered the adulation meaningless. Martin, sensitive enough to know that something was troubling Angelica, gifted her with a certificate to a spa, as if a massage could erase the ongoing fear that was gnawing away constantly at her breast. She, alone, who had devoted herself to bringing life mastery to the world, knew that her life had soured and that some insidious rot was sending tendrils out to foul not only her own prospects, but the lives of all she touched. Far from receding, the desecration penetrated ever deeper.

This was the secret knowledge with which Angelica wrestled as she attempted to escape into sleep every night, rising in the morning only to dress yet again, have breakfast with Charles, teach at the studio and do the occasional media interview or appearance. And until the date of her mammogram arrived, she had no option other than to continue putting one foot ahead of the other. In this way, hour after hour, day after day, she skirted along the edge of a void, yawning and horrific, without the company of a single soul to take pity on her.

PART FIVE

The Grid

1

Three months passed in this way, followed by an extended absence identified publicly as "Angelica's writing sabbatical." Many believed she was out of town, on retreat in Quebec working on a sequel, and the rumor was allowed to persist. A few who absolutely needed to know, Will, Martin and Mira among them, were finally told the truth: Angelica's diagnosis of stage two breast cancer, the lumpectomy, radiation and now chemo. Angelica's first impulse was to call upon the church's emergency courier to let Sophie know, but given the oncologist's assurances that stage two was eminently curable, and Charles' shaming reminder of her tendency to overreact, she decided to at least wait until she got her next set of blood counts back, seeing if things were moving in the right direction. She declined the offer to join a support group, determined to keep the matter private. All the while, she was oddly relieved to have been proven right—that it was not all in her head.

She said nothing to her agent Barrie or to the publisher, who continued to be pleased with how her book was performing. When several emails and phone calls went unanswered, Barrie became nervous that Angelica may have been angrier with her about the lawsuit than she'd let on, and may already be seeking new representation. Barrie called Martin to talk about Angelica, but sworn to secrecy about Angelica's true condition, his response was evasive and unconvincing. And so it was that Barrie concocted a trip to visit Martin, planning to drop by Angelica's unannounced in order to propose she sell into the publisher on

Angelica's behalf not just a sequel, but a multiple book deal. She had, in her arms, a bouquet of red roses and a bottle of white wine.

On the seventh day after Angelica's first of five rounds of chemotherapy, Charles was out and Angelica was finally feeling well enough to answer her own townhouse door. She expected to find the UPS package from NYC's Wigs and Pieces on the front stoop. It was Charles' idea to order the curly, salt and pepper wig from Broadway's favorite theater supplier before she actually needed it. Instead, she found Barrie standing on the stoop, the roses and bottle in hand. Barrie stared at her a beat too long before Martin's car thankfully pulled into the drive and he bounded toward them.

"Barrie, darling, the office said I just missed you!" Martin's words were directed at Barrie, but his eyes were riveted on Angelica, a mixture of embarrassment and apology. But it was too late. Barrie's first look at Angelica said it all.

"These are for you," Barrie said, handing her the roses. A wave of nausea swept through Angelica, who motioned the visitors inside then immediately headed to the guest bathroom. Behind the locked door, she called upon her Angel Chi breathing to calm her body, relieved that the technique held power enough to quell the queasiness, even if her guardian angel remained at large. Still, she could not avoid catching a glimpse of herself in the mirror. Angelica leaned in. Juxtaposed to the portrait that graced her book jacket, there was no comparison. That woman, the author Barrie expected, was vital, commanding. Looking into her dark, sunken eyes, and then turning her pronounced nose left, then right, she no longer appeared brave and bold, but spent. "Get it together, Angelica," she whispered to herself. But over the running water, she could just make out the words passing between the two on the other side of the door.

"...eminently curable...just four more rounds...."

"...fooling yourself, Martin. Did you look into her eyes?...already good as dead."

Horrified, Angelica emerged from the bathroom, quickly ascending the staircase toward her study. She attempted what she hoped was a jaunty wave. "You'll have to excuse me," she managed. "I'm on deadline." Martin and Barrie let themselves out, leaving the wine on the entryway table.

2

Angelica collapsed onto the day bed Charles
had set up for her in her study. Out of habit,
her fingers went to her breast, but now traced
the tender indentation where the cancerous
lump had been removed. While doing so, she
re-ran her new mantra: *Yes, a lymph node had
become involved. Just one.* She closed her eyes,
forcing herself to visualize the one rogue cell
that had busted loose, floating through her
bloodstream, trapped by the node in the last
line of defense. Forced herself to imagine that
there were no others. Just one tiny cell already
banished, the waves of chemicals sweeping
through her bloodstream *merely a precaution*,
that's what the oncologist said. Angelica

understood it all, the survival rates, and the prospect of full recovery. *Just let the chemo run its course and all will be well.*

Charles, late getting home for dinner, enjoyed the bottle of wine he'd found on the entryway table. They chuckled in her retelling of the incident with Barrie and Martin, Angelica offering no resistance when Charles mentioned that he'd invited several actor friends over for a reading of an interesting new script he'd been handed. Angelica headed upstairs, thinking that she could do some work on the sequel that she was sure Barrie had originally come to talk to her about. She imagined the look on Barrie's face when upon completion of her sequel, she fired her and found a new agent. Angelica pulled out her notebook containing random book titles and chapter headings, scratched several out and wrote down a few words. But concentrating diligently as she was, something important kept nagging at her, impatiently waiting for her to finish up and pay it proper attention. When she had finally put her sluggish pen down, she remembered that this matter that needed attending to had something to do with her bloodstream. But instead, she went downstairs to listen to the reading.

Charles' guests were huddled around the dining room table, immersed in their roles. The mayor's top aid was reading the leading role of Casius, not the best actor at the table but an avid theater buff and well-connected. One of the character actors who had supported Charles in numerous roles was there; still employed by the theater company but hedging his bets should Charles get the funding in place to found his own company, as over two beers Charles had been for awhile promising to do. Also among them was an attractive ingénue currently networking her way into Portland's theater scene. But she had come with her lover, an older actress playing the part of the mother. There were breaks in the dialogue when all burst out in laughter, chatted or poured more wine.

Charles noticed that Angelica was more engaged than usual, listening intently from the sofa, refreshing the guest's drinks between scenes, laughing with them. But in truth, she never for a moment forgot that she had that matter of the bloodstream to attend to. At 10, she said her goodbyes and headed back to her study.

3

Ever since the chemo had kicked in, she'd preferred to sleep alone, and Charles, disturbed by her sweats and nausea, was frankly relieved. She changed into her cotton nightgown and picked up a novel by Tolstoy, but quickly put it back down and switched off her oversized bedside lamp. In the dark, her thoughts meandered back through the day, starting with the look on Barrie's face, her own gaunt reflection in the mirror, and then, finally, the matter of the bloodstream that had been nagging at her through it all.

One tiny cell had broken loose, escaped into my veins, was trapped, was excised, but had broken loose, nevertheless. Was there another?

And so what if there were? Of course if a lymph node had caught the first, another would catch the second. That's how it works. The lymph node grabs the rogue cells from the bloodstream. And if the cell evades expulsion, the chemo sweeps through in relentlessly efficient waves. The cancer cells are trapped, killed, absorbed or expelled. My body knows what it's doing. I need only work with my body's natural defenses, take the medicine the oncologist prescribed, attend to her alternative modalities, and of course, my Angel Chi exercises.

She raised herself up, breathing in and out in the distinct pattern of restorative holds and releases she herself had invented, then lying back down again, felt the effects of the chi sending healing energy coursing through her body.

I need only remember to take the medicine and do my practices, throw away my aluminum-based deodorant and give up anything that could possibly be getting in the way of my complete recovery. I feel myself starting to heal already. I am healing.

Her fingers went back to her breast, appreciating the indent that marked the exorcism of the cancerous lump. Switching off the lamp, she marveled at the efficiency of her lymph nodes. But at that very moment, as sudden as a blink, the familiar swill of bitterness rushed up into her throat and she phased out and back again, the interruption of her life flow flooding her with dread. This was not the acute pain of surgery nor the poisonous surge of chemo, but something much more sinister and uninvited that had invaded her body and persisted through it all.

"God no," her fingers rushed first to the indentation, then to her gut. "It's still in me. Back again and again and there is no stopping it."

Suddenly everything was perfectly clear. "Rogue cells, absorbed and expelled!" She mocked herself, even in her rapid descent toward the truth. "This is not about chasing and capturing anything—but a matter of life and of death."

There it was, at last, spoken aloud. What she had seen in Barrie's eyes, it was true—not yet, not completely—for she still had life in her, life enough to feel a lash of anger at Barrie's assertion that she was a dead woman. But with every episode, that life was draining drop by drop out of her, and she could not stop it.

Why kid myself? Barrie knows, Martin knows, anyone but me who looks into my eyes sees that I'm dying—not tomorrow, but in a month maybe two. Deodorant and chemo, breathing techniques and hope—how foolish when seen in this light, dimmed and dimming in the dark shadows cast by truth. Angelica, so present before, so here. And now? She was going, going...

"But where? Where is it that I'm going?" Her cotton gown was cold with sweat and she lay heavy and still, unable to hear anything but a relentless thrumming pulse in her ears.

In the skip of the phase-out, the gone, the nothing—there will be a last time when I go and where will I be then?

But she already knew the answer.

"Was this really death then? Oh please God, no. No! Not this."

She grabbed for the bedside lamp, but her weakened arm scattered the sizeable chunks of Clear and Smoky Quartz, Selenite and salt crystals that had stood guard around the base, a protective grid prescribed by the crystal worker, and her last line of defense. She slumped back down.

"What's the use?" she muttered. "Nothing matters—not now. Not before. Not ever."

She stared into the darkness, and felt the presence of death as never before. Death, indeed. As none of the others knew death to be, didn't want to know, not for her, not for themselves. As Angelica drifted in and out, she caught the distant echoes of animated voices below playing their roles. She had death in her eyes, and yet they played on, no pity for her and no thought of it for themselves. But never mind, for death was as real for them as it was for her. Maybe death would not come as soon to them as to Angelica—the dewy ingénue and aging character actor alike, both who dream only of gaining Charles' admiration—but die they will.

"Blusterers, brutes." The words caught in her throat, the resentment so raw she choked on her own misery. "Every one of us, condemned? This horror—this death—this unspeakable suffering!" She sat up, clutching her chest.

"This cannot be all. Surely, I've missed something." Angelica forced herself to take a deep breath, held it for four counts, and then slowly exhaled through lightly parted lips. Perhaps if she started and ran it all through again from the beginning she would discover where it first went wrong and how things could be put right again.

My heel caught. My breast banged into the corner of the journalist's desk. Yes, it was sore, but it was nothing—a good story, something I could laugh about. But then it didn't go away, or did it? Of course, now I know it didn't. And then there was the bitter taste in my mouth and the first of my episodes. Concern deepened into fear. Then there was Dr. Clark and his diagnosis of fibrotic breasts. Ha. I knew even then that something was terribly wrong, everybody else thinking it was all in my head. The rot, the anguish, the helplessness. Then came the second mammogram, the diagnosis, and all the new doctors, oncologists, breast surgeons, chemo nurses. All the while they were agreeing with one another that my condition was eminently curable, I, Angelica, have been inexorably creeping closer to the edge of the void. Darkness sending its rotten tendrils into my veins. Call it by its true name: Death, Death even while I go pattering on about rogue cells captured, absorbed, cast off. Even while I clutch at my crystals, Death it is. But can this really be it, Death?

Suddenly, the dark room terrified her and she reached for the lamp. The chain that hung high eluded her, slipped through her fingers and she hated the lamp for that, grabbed at it even more frantically and it went flying off the bedside table. As it headed to the floor, Angelica went suddenly limp, certain that at this very moment, death was already upon her.

4

Just as the last of his guests were on their way out, they all heard something hit the floor—a crash—and Charles bolted up the stairs.

"What happened?"

"An accident—it was an accident. The lamp..."

The room was flooded suddenly with overhead light and Charles saw Angelica lying on the bed in the damp cold, exposed and shaking. Her breathing was rapid and she stared blankly into empty space. On the wooden floor lay a chaotic wreck of scattered glass, gemstones and chunks of crystal.

"Angelica, what's going on?"

"Forget it. It fell. That's all." (*Why say more when he'd only tell me it was all in my head. He doesn't get it.*) And Angelica was right about that. Charles bent over to pick up some of the bigger broken pieces then, remembering the guests he'd left standing in the vestibule, hurried out. The front door slammed, one and then another engine started then faded away and, after a long pause, Charles returned.

"My God, Angelica. What the hell's going on? Are you feeling worse?"

"Yes."

"Perhaps we should get a second opinion—Someone at Mass General, or Mayo. Martin must know somebody."

Her lip curled into a vengeful smile and she replied: "No."

Charles sighed, bent down to fix her covers and kiss her goodnight. Repulsed, Angelica clutched at the sides of the bed to keep herself from jerking away.

"Let's hope you can sleep now. I'll turn off the light," Charles said.

"Do."

PART SIX
The Bridge

1

It was a surprise to everyone but Angelica when myeloblasts showed up in her blood count raising cause for heightened alarm. A particularly virulent strain of blood cancer, Myelodysplastic Syndrome, was the diagnosis. There was no more talk of eminent cures and rates of survivability. The church offered no resistance when at Angelica's behest, Charles asked them to dispatch the courier to Sophie. Angelica's note spelled out in detail that she had been offered the option of discontinuing chemo and entering a hospice facility. The chemo, adjusted for the new circumstances, might mitigate some symptoms but was unfortunately guaranteed to introduce others that would be worse. The doctor, a specialist called in to consult from Mass General, was matter of fact as he shared the prognosis. *Chance of cure: zero percent. Chance of remission: zero percent.* His advice: *Go home; Get your affairs in order.*

Angelica took up the offer to stop treatment but refused going to hospice. She opted instead for a private nurse—someone to be on call to monitor vitals and administer pain medications. Fortuitously, this woman, Leticia, happened to be employed by hospice but moonlighted for a succession of VIP patients, passed along in the same manner that qualified English nannies worked their way through the better zip codes. Angelica took grim satisfaction in having been right, but simply could not grasp the logic of it.

I'm dying. All people die. It's part of the human condition to die. We are born, we mature, we die. But the human condition is an abstract, something that happens to "people,"

people taken as a whole, but surely this does not have to do with me.

She, Angelica, was different, unique. Wasn't she her father's special pet, his baby bird, little Ren, the only child allowed behind the pharmacy counter. Her father, dressed in the white starched coat that gave her so much pride, while she waited for him to take her next door for a phosphate. And hadn't she alone been Rena, the one to organize the neighborhood kids to put on backyard plays: Arlene, Jerry, Marcus and Samantha. And she called upon Mira to participate, too, not for a part, but to collect the nickel admission at the folding table Rena set up.

Rena Goodman, alone, was the one girl at summer camp to have an encounter with an angel. And had "humanity" ever soared as high as did her own heart when accepting a dozen red roses from her family after her first starring role? Had anyone ever been so in love as when her college theater director invited her to bed? Nor as tragic as when she discovered that there were others? Had "humanity" ever held such an attentive newborn as Sophie in her arms or taught so many people her new, more effective version of tai chi? *Yes, people are mortal and all people die.* But for Angelica Goodman Banks, with all that she had experienced, all that she had made of herself, it did not make any sense, not in this case. It was quite definitively, horribly inconceivable.

People who are going to die would know it, would understand that dying is their destiny. But it was not so long ago that I was appearing on television, demonstrating the new form of tai chi that I, myself, had created. Where were the inner voices whispering to me about death then? So how could this be happening—to me? It is not possible—and yet it has somehow come about, not just to humanity in general—but to me, in particular. How am I to make sense of it?

Perhaps she had been mistaken—had heard wrong. The blood work had been switched or misread. *Surely a zero percent survival rate is an exaggeration. Dwelling on the worst possible outcome is no more than self-indulgence. I need only replace morbid thoughts with healthier, life-giving ones.*

Angelica made one bold attempt after another to hold the thought of death at bay. But again and again, her effort to stay one step ahead failed. Positive thinking was the first to turn on her, daring to accuse her of a failure of will. But oddly, none of her strategies worked as they should. She called upon her guardian angel to emerge from the shadows, but only the shadows made an advance.

With sudden, chilling clarity, she understood that this had always been the truth of it—everything else an evasion. *Every thought, every meditation, every teaching, and even every angel: they were all smokescreens, futile attempts to obscure the inevitability of death.*

But catching her dark thoughts just as they were spinning out of control, she would berate herself for sinking into morbidity yet again, resolving to try harder.

"There's always the sequel," she reminded herself. "Long after I'm gone, people will still be reading my books. It is why I'm here and why I am still here." And she would not only pull out her notebook and set to work, but tell Martin that she was open to media interviews. Or why not a virtual media tour? About Angel Chi and the upcoming sequel. "But absolutely no mention of my illness. And no TV or webcasts—only phone calls with newspaper reporters and radio talk show hosts."

2

Martin came to the house the day of the virtual tour to handle the logistics, something he had not done for years and would do for no other. She installed her new wig, a little more perfect, a tad shinier, than had been her own salt and pepper curls. Martin, even knowing all the while that she had plummeted to stage four, was relieved to see that it was pretty much the old Angelica who came to the door. They did not address her illness, heading straight to the landline Charles had set up for the tour on the living room table overlooking Casco Bay.

Ivan Dempster had been given the local exclusive, so flattered he neglected to question why she had opted for a phone interview rather than come in person to the newspaper office. The interview went well, Dempster unctuous on the line with the charming local celebrity. This was followed by a carefully orchestrated stream of 2-to-30-minute interviews, sweeping across the country from east to west by time zone. All went well through the eastern seaboard and southeastern states, and deep into the Midwest. But somewhere in the Rockies, Angelica phased out and back again. Still, she didn't skip a beat, the story about encountering her angel repeated so many times she could mouth the words on autopilot.

During commercial break, she sat in desperate silence, attempting to push the horror away, but *It* pushed back and refused to budge. *It* fixed her in its dark gaze and her heart sank. *It* was back and *It* wouldn't let her go. Martin noticed that the gleam had drained out of her eyes and the page of interview notes in her right hand trembled. When the interviewer returned, Angelica turned to Martin with panic in her eyes, and ever the professional, Martin deftly took phone in hand and, feigning technical difficulty, abruptly disconnected the line.

The next 15 minutes were a frenzy of cancellations and apologies, as Martin hit the phones to save face for them both. They lost the entire West Coast. Angelica looking on, more dazed than dismayed, as her prospects unraveled. One after another, a flight of phase-outs fluttered through her consciousness, and in the end, *It* was the only thing that held her attention.

"It's alright," Martin said after his last difficult phone call. "We can reset the West Coast when you're feeling better." He tried his best not to let on how distressed he was by the incident, confronting the truth that both he and his astute prodigy had misjudged her state so acutely. As he gathered his things to leave, Angelica rallied, sad that she had let her good friend down. But as soon as he left, a greater sorrow consumed her.

Her attempt to outsmart *It* had failed. Now there was nowhere left to hide from *It*. And even more terrifying, there was nothing *It* wanted her to do, nothing to try or aspire to. All *It* wanted from her was her full attention. *It* was all there was, and beyond *It* there was nothing.

3

The torment was insufferable so she had no choice but to find another way. Hiding, ignoring, pushing back—none of these had worked. But what if she were, instead, to face *It* head on...not do the sequel about healing and life mastery the Angel Chi way, but instead, write a book about death and dying.

Surrender. Acceptance. Chi, after all, is not only about the light. Isn't all this I'm experiencing simply the yin to the yang? How stupid I've been not to have seen the truth of it staring me in the face all along: an embrace of the shadow as well as the light—the courage to become whole.

She grabbed a new notebook in which to capture her new book title *Angel Chi: Making Peace with Shadows,* buoyed by the secret knowledge that this must be the meaning of all that she had endured. But before a single word was committed to paper, her conviction collapsed under the weight of *It. It* was everywhere she turned, even in her notebook, relentless in its power to undermine and destroy.

Even so, in this liminal bridge in time between the end of her last chemo and before the onslaught of even nastier symptoms, she did not take to bed. Instead, she got up with Charles every morning, throwing on the pretty robe Mira had sent upon hearing her original diagnosis, eager to see him to the door. Alone in the townhouse, she would sometimes make her way to the closet, find the box that contained the high heels she had worn on her book tour. Jimmy Choos, pointy-toe pumps in black leather, bought as reward for landing the book deal. $875 out of her generous advance. The deal was negotiated by Martin and Barrie on the promise of what Angelica could deliver: the key to self-mastery. How proud she had been striding into the television studios, radio stations, in and out of limousines and fancy hotels in her Jimmy Choos. People who knew recognized the shoes, understood what they meant. That she was Somebody.

Now, she looked down at them with a rueful smile. She recalled walking into that newspaper interview in Denver, so pumped she had forgotten to kick them off. Her heel caught in the carpeting, she banged her chest against the side of the desk, and over and over again in her tortured imagination, the lump that had been there for years—persistent, unwavering, and patiently waiting—broke open. In the blink of an eye, the encapsulated cancer cells charged forth and were now circulating, multiplying throughout her circulatory system. Angelica turned the shoes over in her hand, her thin fingers tracing the scuffs and scratches the soles had suffered over the course of the tour. She then put them on, walking the hall, taunting fate by descending and ascending the staircase that was covered in thick, loopy carpeting, stopping before mirrors to strike an Angel Chi pose. *How foolish I look, tottering about in these ridiculously high heels, the very shoes that cost me my life.*

After, she frequently headed to the guest room, the room that had once been Sophie's. From the bed, tucked between Sophie's favorite childhood teddy bear and a heart-shaped pillow, Angelica plucked the latest of her beloved daughter's letters from the stack.

"Oh no, Mom. The letter from the courier just got here. Of course, I want to come home. In fact, I can't get home to be with you soon enough. They say that the bridge will be reopened shortly, as soon as they can clear the damage from the avalanche. Hang in there, mom. I love you so much. See you soon. I promise."

Despite repainted walls and rearranged furniture, the room was still Sophie's. Angelica reached for a carton of sweaters from the pile of boxes in the closet, bringing pink cashmere up to her nose, the faint scent of white jasmine warming her heart. Another box contained the scrapbooks Angelica had put together for Sophie from infancy, through childhood, adolescence and young adulthood. She pulled out the album containing Sophie's high school years, the one with the puffy pink cover they had picked out together on her 16th birthday. Angelica opened the cover and an 8-by-10 photo of the two of them doing tai chi together in Master Chen's matching black tee-shirts tumbled out. She grabbed for it, seeing that a corner had been creased. The album had obviously been opened and shut carelessly by who—Sophie? Her husband? Sophie's friends? She turned the pages, increasingly outraged at the number of photos that were torn, missing or hastily reinstalled upside down. Diligently, Angelica unfolded the bend and one by one set each of the others right. When she was done, it occurred to her that with Sophie coming home, she should restore her room to its original state, beginning with hanging the pink sweater in the closet and putting the furniture back the way Sophie had left it. When Charles came home, there were boxes, nightstands, chairs and knickknacks scattered everywhere, a terrible mess he was expected to help her put to rights.

"What were you thinking," he protested. "She's a married woman. She's not coming to stay." Angelica protested. They argued. Doors slammed. She cried. But it was all such a relief because none of this had anything to do with *It*.

Defiant, she picked up a too-high stack of scrapbooks, the top album scattering to the floor. Charles grabbed the rest of the albums from her thin arms, shouting "Put them down, you're going to drop these, too." But before she could respond, *It* was back. *It* flew across the room, a fleeting shadow, and against her will, she phased out. When she came back, she saw that not only was the shadow still present, but had penetrated her core. What did any of what they'd argued about matter?

Was it the truth, then, that for the sake of these Jimmy Choo heels, I gave up my life? It's all quite simply too stupid to be true. And yet, here I am, and here It is, she moaned inwardly.

She took the heels off and walked barefoot back to the study, threw herself on the day bed, and beside her, beneath her, on top of her, everywhere she tossed and everywhere she turned, there *It* was. There was no escaping *It*, nothing more she could do but give it the attention it demanded of her. She lay there, gazing upon it with endless dread.

PART SEVEN

Hallway

1

Anyone who noticed her absence, including her editor at the publishing house, was told that Angelica was hard at work on her sequel. But for those who knew the real story, Angelica's freefall from stage two to four was inconceivable. Nobody, not even Charles, ever spoke to her about the future. Martin hated doing so, but nevertheless participated in relentless conversations with Barrie about the legal and financial implications of what they had begun referring to as Angelica's "condition."

Mira, still pained about having been marginalized early on when she felt she could have done something about it, now resented both her sister's and Charles's sudden neediness. Nevertheless, she began making plans to come out to Portland sooner rather than later. (Charles told her he not only needed help with Angelica, but with the business of running the studio and, in a stage whisper, "succession.") How long the stay she, nobody, knew for certain—weeks/months? She decided she would need to buy a larger suitcase.

Sophie also made plans, but her plans included dealing with rural transportation officials and bridge construction managers who had been saying "next week, next week" for over a month. She was genuinely sincere in her desire to get home to the mother she loved as quickly as possible. However, she was less anxious than she might otherwise have been, refusing to believe—despite her mother's horrifically detailed letter—that this was anything more than the latest of Angelica's attention-getting attempts. Justin suggested that by the time Sophie made it home, everything would be just as it was before. When her faith wavered, they prayed together.

As for Angelica, without knowing how or when it had come about, she experienced every interaction, every kindness, every expression of concern as the thinnest of veils masking the only real question on every mind, including hers. "Is this ever going to end?"

With each passing day, Angelica's sleep became that much more elusive, the aches in her bones more pronounced and her nausea more acute. During her increasingly frequent visits, Nurse Leticia, now "Letty," efficiently dispensed a variety of prescribed medications, steroids and narcotics that distracted Angelica with new dulling sensations. In short order, Angelica found the haze of anguished confusion they induced more unbearable than the original pain. She began refusing all but the everyday remedies—the aspirin, the Maalox. But then again, even something as previously taken for granted as going to the bathroom now included its own unavoidable regimen of fibers, gels, pills and suppositories. When food turned revolting, a nutritionist was consulted, but to no avail. Only Letty knew which flavor of jello Angelica could best tolerate, and when she was ready to be helped to the toilet. It was no longer okay with Angelica when Letty had to excuse herself to go to her hospice job, and Letty was reluctant to leave her. By the time Letty suggested that they remedy this by formalizing her care under the official hospice umbrella, Angelica, as well as Charles, were relieved.

The move to formalize hospice care was timely, for Angelica could no longer be certain of making it down the hall to the bathroom, even with assistance. She was ashamed of her neediness, embarrassed for Letty, who kept a supply of freshly laundered uniforms in the closet should an accident occur. The stench of it, the awkwardness, the indignity would have been unbearable, but for the matter-of-fact way in which Letty produced the bedpan, gently lifted her into position, and then after, the feel of warm moist cloths against Angelica's tender skin. That even this odious torture could be mitigated by such ordinary kindness was a comfort.

2

One morning, Letty downstairs preparing a bowl of lime jello, Angelica managed to get herself down the hall. Her robe soiled and she threw it off, stumbling back to the study naked, collapsing into the armchair beside her bed. Angelica stared down miserably at her wasted body, bone-thin fingers tracing the twisted ridges of sinew on each one of her shrunken thighs. Just then, she heard the toilet flush, water running and the faint sound of scrubbing. Letty appeared at the door, and with a breezy stride, brought a fresh robe to Angelica. Letty smelled of clean, cheerful lime, as if about to burst out in song. Tenderly, she guided her charge's thin arms into the sleeves and carefully arranged the robe to cover her exposed body.

"Letty," Angelica said, in such a mournful tone, the hospice nurse worried that even the thought of a song had been insensitive given Angelica's fragile state.

"This must be awful for you, Letty. All the disgusting things you have to do for me. Please forgive me. I just can't help myself."

Letty smiled. "That's what's upsetting you, *Mi Tesoro*? But that's what hospice is for. It's what I do." Letty left as lightly as she had come and then after a few minutes, returned again with the bowl of green jello. She stayed with her while Angelica did her best to swallow a couple of spoonfuls, then Letty started to clear it away.

"Letty. Don't go."

"Do you need something, *Mi Tesoro*?"

"My feet...my feet are cold." Letty grabbed some thick white cotton socks from the drawer, and after gently tugging them into place, gave each toe an affectionate squeeze.

"Letty, do you have to go yet?"

Letty who had worked the night shift with hospice was meant to meet up with friends for a cappuccino at Starbucks, but they could wait. She smiled.

"It's just that it felt so good," Angelica said.

"Would you like a foot massage?" Letty took Angelica's right foot, and began kneading. For the first time for as long as she could remember, Angelica felt only pleasure, no pain. They stayed this way for quite a while, until Angelica fell asleep, and Letty left to catch up with her friends.

From that point on, Letty always made sure to have a fresh pair of socks nearby for her, and while she massaged Angelica's feet, they would talk. Not just about prescriptions and flavors of jello, but about their lives. Letty had grown children and a number of grandchildren. Letty empathized about Sophie. Among her own concerns: there was a difficult daughter-in-law, and a grandchild having reading problems. Some family lived close by, but her favorite, her youngest son, had gone off to UMaine two hours away. She was proud, but she missed him terribly. When asked, she shared that she had trained for hospice after her husband passed, finding that she had a natural, effortless inclination for caregiving. In turn, Angelica told her about Angel Chi and about her book. Angelica loved their conversations, the simplicity and goodness with which Letty approached everything, be it stories about her family, or emptying the bedpan. Aside from Letty, the thought of people continuing to live full, robust lives upset Angelica, but with Letty it was different. Her strength, her kindness and her simplicity, it all came together in such a way as to put Angelica at ease.

CAROL ORSBORN

Of everything, what Angelica detested most was "the lie." When Martin came to visit, he attempted to cheer her up with the clipping of a good review her book had received, and occasionally, some news about mutual acquaintances. (Without, of course, mention of Master Chen, who continued to be angry with her.) Charles, and all the others, spoke of her illnesses as if it were a bad case of the flu, rather than something terminal. Mira was constantly forwarding stories about mitigating symptoms including consuming massive doses of B12 and large quantities of oranges. Martin made it his business to seek out Hail Mary drug trials and experimental protocols. Angelica turned down the desperate pursuit of a bone marrow transplant at her age—the very procedure that had been captured in Annie Liebowitz's revolting deathbed photo of lover Susan Sontag, bloated with steroids and covered with sores. In a late night argument, Charles charged that as she had been refusing everything recommended, if Angelica died, it would be her own damn fault. She didn't have the strength to fight back.

Regardless of her best efforts and wishes, all she or any of them could anticipate was the inexorable degradation of her dwindling life, more pain, more suffering. They enacted sincere concern, or scolded out of discomfort, but they were torturing her with their attempts to force her into compliance with the lie. Meals she could not eat arrived on the front stoop regularly, sent over by Justin's family and well-meaning church members from Third Baptist, pledged to secrecy but unable to refrain from offering their prayers. Barrie sent her uplifting books accompanied by funny cards that read "Get Well Soon." That this lie was being foisted upon her in the last days of her life, a falsehood that trivialized the enormity of this dreadful passage, was all the more unconscionable. What she wanted to do was scream: "You selfish, stupid people—every single one of you—Stop pretending. I'm dying, so stop the lying." But she kept her anger to herself. She knew it wasn't personal—that they were simply incapable of facing the enormity of death head-on, reducing it to something more manageable, if unusually disagreeable. When caught off guard, she saw that they averted their eyes or pursed their lips. Angelica searched their eyes and their actions for pity, or any acknowledgment that something horrific was happening to her. But each, in his or her own way, lacked the will to comprehend what she was enduring. When their feeble attempts to help failed, they distanced themselves, going through the motions while counting the minutes until they could escape.

Angelica could not wait for the others to leave and for Letty to take up her curled toes. While Letty kneaded, patted and tugged, Angelica was able to let go. Patient and strong, Letty's fingers went on massaging her feet, sometimes through a good part of the day or night, until Angelica fell asleep.

3

Sometimes Angelica asked her to leave—
Letty's son was on spring break or a
grandchild needed a lesson.

"*Mi Tesoro*, please don't worry about me.
You're sick and you need me." Letty, alone,
felt no need to lie. She had faced many deaths
in her time, and knew death for what it was.
Dying to her was as real, as tangible as life
itself. And while she pitied each of those, in
turn, whose time had come, she did not fear
for them. On one occasion, Angelica first
begged then demanded that she go home, but
Letty was firm.

"We're all going to die, Angelica. Why are
you special?" She meant no disrespect by this,

and Angelica suddenly understood. This was Angelica's turn to be the suffering patient, and tomorrow, it would be someone else's. Eventually, someone would be called upon to help Letty herself, someone to massage her feet and change her bedpan.

Between Letty's shifts, when Charles stepped in, Angelica endured his reports from the outside world and his forced cheerfulness. But all she really wanted—craved—was his pity. She wanted him to cry for her as she had cried for Sophie when she had the mumps or a stomach ache, cradling her in her arms, kissing her forehead and singing to her. She knew that Charles could play the part if he so wished, but he could not—after all these years—think of Angelica in this way—needy, out of control—for more than a fleeting moment. It was never going to happen, but still, it was what she yearned for.

She wanted this from Martin, too, thought that an honest relationship was what they had, and yet when he came to visit, he always came to cheer her up. One afternoon, he arrived in a particularly jovial mood.

"Great news, Angelica. Your book has been selected as Grand Prize winner of the Nautilus Book Awards." The best part about the reward, however, was that it came bundled with the opportunity for an even greater prize: the redemption of the cruelly postponed interview with *The New York Times*.

"They asked to have you come to New York to interview you in person, but Charles and I decided it best to offer them Skype. Charles has a great idea. We call in the make-up and lighting techs from the theater to set the scene. Of course, I can stand by with the disconnect switch. Given the upside, it's worth the risk, don't you think? This means your book still has a shot at number one."

She feigned enthusiasm, and against every honest impulse, agreed. And for this, for the living of the lies that were spoiling the last of her days, and for the falsehood within her that she was too weak to resist, Angelica felt the greatest self-pity of all.

PART EIGHT
The Visit

1

Angelica blinked against the beam of sun streaming through a crack beneath the shade. She knew it was morning because today it was Mira at her side, not Letty or Charles. Mira sprang into action, raising the shade and straightening the bedcovers. Angelica stared at her sister expressionless, not caring whether it was day or night, or whether the comforter was crumpled or smooth. *What difference did any of it make?* Nothing at all had changed about the only things that really mattered: the raw sores inside her mouth that made swallowing difficult, the gnawing nausea interrupted periodically by spears of pain. But above all, the incessant draining away of her life force, not yet gone, but going; the rot of death the only real thing in the room.

"How about some tea?" Mira asked in a cheerful tone. Having ascertained that the bitter taste in Angelica's mouth was not a matter of heartburn, she had succeeded in reintroducing green tea into the menu, but it was too late. *Mira wants to show off that she's in charge now,* Angelica thought. But she just said "No."

"Can I help you to the chair?"

She wants to make the bed and neaten up the room, and I'm the one out of order, a stink, a stain she wants to rub out. But Angelica simply answered: "Please go." Mira went on tidying the room as if she hadn't heard her sister. After awhile, Angelica motioned to her.

"Where's my watch? I need my watch."

"What for?

"When did Letty leave? Is Charles up yet?"

"Letty left awhile ago. You do remember that today is Letty's day off? And Charles is sleeping in. He was up late last night but said I could get him up if you asked for him. Should I?"

"No. But I could use some tea. That's it. Can you get me tea?"

Mira turned to leave, and Angelica was suddenly face to face with the fear that she was about to be abandoned. Desperate to keep her sister from leaving, she searched for a ploy.

"Mira, get me the Advil." Mira complied, it certainly wouldn't hurt. *But if only Angelica weren't being so hard-headed about the real painkillers hospice was authorized to dispense this would all be so much easier on everybody.*

Angelica attempted to swallow the pills, but with the open sores in her mouth and throat, she gagged. Mira offered to run to the kitchen and bring her the liquid version, but Angelica just stared at her. They both knew it was too late for that, that the Advil, liquid or not, was a joke. *If only the pain would go away*, Angelica sighed to herself. *Why so much pain?* Angelica's sigh turned into a moan and Mira rushed back to her.

"Where's the tea?" Angelica nearly shouted, suddenly wanting urgently to be alone. "The tea!"

Mira left the room reluctantly, listening to moans trailing after her down the stairs. But it wasn't the pain escaping with her breath, unbearable as it was, that was causing Angelica to tremble. It was the relentless repetition of days and nights, the endless procession of hopeless remedies and unsatisfying interactions that hounded her as she waited. Anxious for it to come already. For what to come? *For shadows. For death. Oh my God, what am I thinking? No! Not wish for death—wish for anything but death!*

Mira returned, balancing a cup, a spoon rest and stirrer, a strainer and the steaming pot of green tea on a tray. Angelica simply gazed at her, with a peculiarly vague look that disturbed Mira as much as anything that had transpired since she had arrived. It was as if Angelica had forgotten who Mira was. Sensing alarm, Angelica gathered herself sufficiently to reach out for the cup. After swallowing a painful sip, she asked her sister to help her freshen up. Mira brought over the handi-wipes, refreshed the water in the bowl Angelica used for brushing her teeth. Angelica splashed some of the water into her palm to cool down her head, repulsed by the feel of the patchwork of bare spots and flaccid salt and pepper strands of hair still exhibiting the effects of chemo, and the silver fuzz struggling to fill in the spaces.

She had not looked down at her body since the day she'd stumbled naked down the hall back to her chair, repulsed by her own sinewy limbs and sunken chest. Eyes averted, she was enduring the removal of her soiled gown and the installation of its freshly laundered replacement. She was now ready for the overstuffed armchair, Mira bearing the dead weight of her body for the transfer. The tray remained on the nightstand nearby, and for a moment, Angelica anticipated taking another sip, forgetting that now each swallow caused her pain. But even before she could manage to get the cup of tea to her lips, the familiar bitter taste swelled up from deep inside her and hot liquid spilled from the cup onto her fresh gown. She asked Mira to take the tray and go.

2

So it went. A tendril of hope, crushed beneath the wheels of her slow-moving despair. Not just once, but over and over again. She was alone, and she dreaded it; but when others came, it was even more oppressive. Maybe it was time for the drugs, after all. She would speak with Letty about it. But where was Letty?

The minutes passed, each one longer than the last. Now an hour, Mira floating in and out, busy with something or other. Then, a knock at the door. It was Martin, matching Mira's efficient energy, reinforcing the troops with good news. No, the *New York Times* had not set a new date for the interview after they had been forced to cancel the Skype session at the last minute when Angelica began throwing up. (He never did tell Angelica that the interview would never be rescheduled because it was now considered to be "old news.") But there was something even better. Martin had prevailed upon a high-level contact to bring about the miraculous: a home visit by a specialist from no less than Mayo, who happened to be in town.

"This afternoon! Today! I know it's an ordeal, Angelica, but this doctor is involved with a promising new trial." He paused and shivered involuntarily, then, with unintended emphasis, added: "Gosh, it's cold out there." Mira rushed off to get something hot, as if once Martin got his bouillon, everything would reset to normal. On the way, Mira roused Charles to tell him about this promising development.

"Did you sleep well?" Martin asked as soon as Mira had left, but Angelica could not move herself to answer. *Will there never be an end to all the lies?* But Martin persisted.

"After your doctor's visit, I'd like to bring by some of our friends from the theater. We'll be heading on to a fundraiser. Some disease. Charles is invited, of course, and they've been asking about you." Angelica knew that of necessity, as the weeks turned into months, the circle of those who had been let in on her dreadful secret had expanded. But only to include those who could be trusted to keep her condition secret. For a moment, Angelica was swept up in something akin to the prospect of normalcy, then remembered that, of course, Martin was in public relations. *He's trained to lie. Gets paid for it.*

Martin was still chatting away when Mira and a rumpled Charles in t-shirt and jeans appeared at the door. Charles bent down to kiss Angelica on the forehead, acting as though he'd been up for quite a while; sorry he hadn't been there to greet Martin earlier.

Angelica took it all in, Charles' leading man demeanor, reeking of charisma. She took in the fleshiness of his exposed arms, and her stomach turned. She detested the look of him, the smell of him. And the touch of his kiss left her with a flush of hatred.

Nothing had changed with him, not really. Not since he long ago determined that if she did not do exactly as he said, she was herself to blame for any of the misfortune that should come about. Charles did what he had to for her, did it so efficiently and, in his own mind, lovingly, while suffering the unavoidable fact that Angelica was, even now, still Angelica.

"She says no to everything," Charles responded to the offer for a house call, as if Angelica weren't lying there, two feet away. "Maybe she'll stop being so damn bull-headed and give this doctor a fair hearing."

"Of course she will," said Mira. "What time can we expect him?"

Angelica smiled grimly, not bull-headed, bull-dozed. With the three of them aligned against her, she failed to muster sufficient will to protest.

It was for her own good, Charles told her later. In fact, everything he ever did or would do was for her, an assertion so ludicrous that she took it at face value as signifying exactly the opposite.

3

The specialist arrived precisely at 3 p.m. Mira had folders of lab reports, copies of x-rays and doctor's notes to share, but the specialist, whose phone calls were invariably answered promptly, had already been in touch with Angelica's Portland oncologist. He did listen to her heart, palpate her abdomen and check the swelling in her ankles. But mostly he examined the documents, speaking as though the issue that confronted them was merely a matter of hormone therapy and immune response stimulation, rather than of life or death. *Life or death?* This was the only question that interested Angelica, but rather than hope for an answer, she was already bracing herself for yet another proposal for a long-shot remedy.

And here it was. Angelica was, indeed, a possible candidate for a first phase trial. Of course, there were risks in the protocol—and in fact, no guarantee that Angelica would be admitted. That would depend on the results of her blood work. But yes, there was a chance of a remission. Angelica sat up, her eyes suddenly bright with hope. Mira, rather than buoyed by Angelica's response, sank noticeably. Later, Mira told Charles that he had been mistaken. The look on Mira's face had been relief not disappointment—really. But in truth, the prospect of a prolonged, pathetic attempt at a cure rather than a renewed attempt to alleviate Angelica's current pain had been too much for her.

She needn't have worried about the attempt at a cure, for Angelica's glint of optimism was soon gone. By later that very afternoon, even before the blood work came back disqualifying her, Angelica had reentered despair. She lay on the same bed, staring at the same walls, feeling the same nausea, tasting the same bitter swill. In a desperate attempt to escape the pain, she fell into a fitful sleep.

4

When she woke, there were shadows in the room and she heard cheerful voices downstairs. Charles came into the study first, dressed for the fundraiser in the tux he had invested in years ago. Angelica noted critically that it was too snug across his belly. The brief hope for normalcy that had flitted through at the prospect of visitors was gone, and she resented the surfacing of the tux, and, in fact, any signs of life outside her four walls. But of course, she now remembered that she had not only agreed to Martin's request for the visit, but had urged Charles to accompany the others to the event. Mira emerged from the shadows to help Charles move Angelica from the bed to the armchair, Charles leaving to carry in chairs from the guest room. Mira neatly installed the wig on Angelica's exposed head. Just as she was placing the shawl she'd knit for her around Angelica's gaunt shoulders, Martin joined them, pleased with having arranged this visit, but feeling somewhat guilty too, knowing that the old Angelica would have loved to go to the fundraiser herself. In fact, the fundraiser would have probably been at the Angel Chi studio and she and Charles would have likely served as co-hosts.

As Charles went to fetch the others, Martin sat down on the edge of the bed, the only one among her friends afforded this intimacy. Stroking Angelica's hand, he asked how she was doing, not that he thought there was anything new to learn, nor that he expected a response, but because it was the only logical preamble to the words he felt compelled to share with her.

"The last thing I want to do is go to this fundraiser. If I had the choice, I'd much rather stay with you eating popcorn and watching TV. Have you seen *Mozart in the Jungle* yet? I can find it for you on Netflix. You're going to love it!"

"Did you say *Mozart of the Jungle?* I love that show!" The ingénue new to town, Betsy, arrived at the open study door, relieved for having been cued with just the right line. Close behind was Kenneth, the character actor who, along with most of the others who came to visit, had been part of Charles' script-reading circle. Of necessity, having had front row seats to Angelica's decline, they had been among the first outside the innermost circle to be told. Stephen, the mayoral aide, entered with a stunning teenager on his arm. She sported the same long, curly hairstyle as Sophie had at her age. The girl's silk gown showed a disconcerting amount of skin, upsetting for not only being age-inappropriate, but for providing too stark a contrast to Angelica's wasted flesh. The girl was introduced as Annette, Stephen's daughter, taking his wife's place when at the last minute the wife had come down with a cold. She exuded vitality and impatience, resentful that her ticket to the glamorous fundraiser had come bundled with a forced confrontation with sickness and death.

Last in, trembling as she crossed the threshold, was Sarah, the one friend Angelica could normally count on to share both intimate stories and empathy. Over lunch or coffee, they had supported each other through career challenges, wayward children and disappointing marriages. The fact that Sarah owned the local bookstore was both a plus and a minus. The plus was that she had been a great supporter when Angelica had decided to write a book, and more so, when her book hit the bestseller list. The minus was that between their equally busy schedules, the good friends often had to postpone so that their intended weekly get-togethers stretched to once a month or longer. Truthfully, the distance between visits had accelerated at about the same pace as her illness. "Doing diseases," by Sarah's own admission, was not her "strong point." Today, she had an acutely frightened demeanor, her panicked eyes capable of inspiring terror in their own right. Still, Angelica was happiest to see her, feeling that Sarah was the only one of her girlfriends who grasped the horror of what she was going through.

They took their places around the room, Charles, Annette and Sarah preferring to stand. There was a moment of awkward silence before one of them—the ingénue—thought of something to say.

"So, have you seen it, *Mozart in the Jungle?*"

"What a great piece of work!" Stephen replied. "Gael García Bernal is brilliant as the conductor."

"You don't think he's a bit, oh I don't know, hammy?" Charles retorted, leading to an argument between them that spread like wildfire around the room with everybody offering an opinion. The banter died out as quickly as it had begun, leaving them once again in silence.

"What do you think?" Martin directed to Angelica. At first, she was confused by his question, but feeling everybody's eyes on her, said glumly:

"I haven't seen it."

Stephen said he thought, in fact, it was the best series on television. To which his daughter noticeably rolled her eyes. Thus ensued a passionate conversation about the pros and cons of various shows, exactly the kind of bandying that takes place sooner or later at most parties.

Mid-sentence, Charles glanced over at Angelica, and abruptly stopped. The others turned to Angelica and the room fell silent. Angelica was glaring at them, eyes bright with fury. Something had to be done, but even Martin, the consummate public relations professional, froze. The very essence of the lie, the truth they all feared, was in danger of being exposed. Annette, young and impulsive, was just as eager as the rest to keep the lie well-hid, but in her impatience, she laid it bare.

"Can we go?" she said to her father. "This is making us late."

Charles stood up to kiss Angelica on the forehead, accompanied by a chorus of goodbyes, and good wishes. By the time he finished, all were gone.

Angelica hugged the shawl close around her, thinking that she was feeling the chi at last begin to stir. But she too quickly realized that it was not the resumption of her life force, but rather relief that the lie had departed with them. She looked down at her painfully bony fingers clutching at the wool wrap, and knew that nothing at all had changed. *It* was still with her, relentless in its persistence. No, not just persistent, worsening.

After they left, Mira flitted in and out, but Angelica's attention remained focused solely on the encroaching void, terrifying in its inescapable nothingness. Once more, time stalled and death was her only true companion.

"Yes. Send her up when she gets here," Angelica responded to a question. Letty's day off was finally coming to an end.

PART NINE

Bed

1

Upon his late night return, Charles was met at the door by Letty who waved him upstairs. Thinking Angelica was asleep, he settled heavily into the armchair and studied her wasted shape beneath the covers. Her eyelids fluttered open and closed again, but it was too late. They both knew she was awake.

"I'm going to stay with you awhile. Okay?"

"No. Just let me be."

"Is it bad, Angelica? Should I get Letty?" Angelica knew that was code for administering the narcotics she had consistently rejected after her first dispiriting encounter. Finding her pain unbearable, he took it upon himself to fetch Letty and then retired for the night.

Angelica consented to a double-dose of bitter liquid, assured by Letty that this one was non-narcotic, powerful, but not addictive. To Letty's experienced eye it was clear that she fell quickly into a restless sleep. But not so for Angelica. She experienced every horrifying second of the ensuing hours, eyes closed, but lucid and terrified. The yawning void that chemo had torn open months ago had grown only broader and deeper. The larger horror was the insistent pressure of an overpowering force pressing her inexorably toward the brink. She clung desperately to the edge, but with its final shove, she plunged in. The relentless force thrust Angelica and her pain deeper and deeper into the darkness. The force was unbearable, torturous. She grappled with it, terrified of being released, yet mustered every ounce of her will to give up, to be done with it at last. But the force was resisting her every attempt to yield. Suddenly, her grip on the force gave way and she plummeted back into her bed, eyes opened wide in silent terror. Letty was sitting quietly in the armchair, a fresh pair of cotton socks on her lap. The pain was fully present.

"Not now," Angelica whispered. "I want to be alone."

It was 4 a.m., but Letty had things she could be doing downstairs.

"Are you sure?"

"Yes."

2

As soon as she was alone, Angelica coiled into a ball beneath the covers and broke into sobs. Attempting to muffle her desperation, she sent her tears deep into the pillow, suffocating with sorrow and anger. *When will it end? All the anguish, the lies, the pain, the helplessness. Where's my angel, her shimmering wings and unconditional love? How could she abandon me when I most need her? Where is compassion, where is mercy? Where is God?*

"What did I do to deserve this?" she spoke the words out loud. "How could You be so merciless, so cruel? For what cause, for what purpose?"

There was no reply, but she knew that it was the silence itself that constituted the answer—the only response there could be. A spear of pain struck her side, but she stifled these cries, too.

"Come on then, God. You want to hurt me? Do it again, I dare you! Ha! But why, God? Didn't I always do my best? All the good I did—You owe me. You all owe me. Oh God, why do you hate me so?"

Then, sudden as a gasp, all was still. No more stifled cries or muffled screams; instead, only the elongated pause between inhale and exhale as Angelica bolted upright into clarity. Silence was not the answer. Silence was the question, the question only she could answer.

What are you hoping for?

"What is it that I'm hoping for? For the suffering to end. To live."

To be alive—yes. That was her answer and her prayer.

But how? In what way?

215

"Go back to the way things were before—joyful, loving, peaceful."

You were joyful, loving and peaceful—when?

Thoughts flooded her, starting with her earliest memories. Little Ren, riding in the back seat of her parent's dark green Pontiac, a beam of sunlight captured in the palm of her hand. Yes, that had been a purely joyful moment. There were other memories as well, peaceful, playful encounters she had forgotten from long ago. These she could go back to happily, live over and over again. But of course, Little Ren grew into Rena. There was her father's starched white coat, the pharmacy counter, but where was Mira when Rena had sipped phosphates with her father, from her own straw but a shared glass? And what of Lillian, Rena forcing herself to recall her mother, scanning their life together as if telling a story about strangers. There had been happiness, trips to department stores and birthday parties on the patio, but it seemed as if it all belonged to someone else, the young child she had left behind long ago, along with her given name.

The story line surged forward. Her first opening night in New York, her first lobster in Portland, her marriage to Charles, birthing Sophie, studying with Master Chen: All that had converged to create Angelica Goodman Banks, the woman she was today.

All well and good. But where is the girl who had held sunlight in her hand? Where there had once been joy, what? Pleasure? Popularity? The appearance of success?

As the pages turned, picking up speed, happinesses were scattering hither and thither, this one exposed as superficial, that one but a shadow. None were what they had seemed to be, and some had turned foul.

But even all that was long ago. Then what of the pages still wet with ink? She had thrived under the tutelage of Master Chen. Surely, there had been life lived to the full then: mastery, respect—and hope? But that had been beaten out of her one dreadful day, just as surely as Master Chen had been left in the alley to die. Not long after, she had become Angelica, mistress of angels, a joy not born of freedom, but reactivity, and so not true joy at all. Still, there were moments of contentment. Sophie had been pure happiness. But then, even that love had turned to pain. Angel Chi and the publication of her book, as it rose toward the top of the bestseller list. But when it stalled? The Lawsuit? The faster the pages turned, the less goodness there was to find.

So, Charles. How passionately in the beginning Angelica had longed for true love, a marriage that would endure in sickness and in health. But long before the sickness set in, it was only the two of them who had endured, not the joy. She, who suffered his self-indulgence, his lack of control, his incompetence. He, who refused to leave center stage gracefully, turning every act of their life into either a comedy or tragedy, and it sickened her.

How they envied and admired us, those students and readers, the theater-goers and critics. I thought we were getting somewhere, that I was becoming Somebody but all the while I was inching closer and closer to the abyss. Now the final chapter of the book of life is being writ, not in chi and life force, but with shadows and with death. And it is death that will have the final word.

What has it all been about, this thing called life? If it is all to go by so quickly, all brutality and disappointment with but flashes of joy, flutters of peace? And then, in the end, only to die in pain and suffering? It makes no sense. Unless, unless—What if it were me? What if I did it all wrong? Not at the very beginning, there was joy in the beginning. But what if, after that, all along, choice by choice, I failed to do the right thing?

Angelica clutched her chest, contorted with white-hot pain. But as suddenly as the burning began, it stilled, and in its place, new questions smoldered. *How could that possibly be true? Didn't I always do everything I could? My best?* And thus Angelica extinguished the only sensible explanation that could possibly have laid to rest the ultimate conundrum: *Why do we live if only to die?*

So now what? What is it that you want? To go back to how things were before? Angelica, the author of her life, tearing open the pages of The New York Times, searching for the critical review of her life work. How will I be judged? She paused at the gate of judgment, but rather than guilt, there was protest. "For I am innocent. I did nothing wrong. Explain Yourself, God. Defend Yourself! Why do we live only to die? What does it all mean?" Then, when there were no more tears left, she became suddenly aware that her pillow had grown moist and cold. She turned on her side and stared at the wall, asking herself over and over again the only question that persisted. "Why?"

Quieter now, but insistent, the question nagged her for a response, but she had none to give. Perhaps she hadn't always lived as she should after all, but no. This was just her illness speaking, not the truth. For whatever her shortcomings and omissions, she did not deserve this.

PART TEN
Wall

1

So the days and weeks passed, Angelica turned toward the wall, thinking things through but coming to no satisfying resolution. The only real change was that, at her request, she had been moved from the bed to the armchair. When she had refused to be lifted back to bed even to sleep, there had been a discussion between Mira, Charles and Letty. The decision was made to bring in a zero gravity recliner, one Letty knew about that was based on an ergonomic design used by astronauts. Letty had a source (which turned out to be the daughter of a client who had recently passed). They were offered the option of buying or renting. After further conversation, much of it difficult, the determination was made to rent. Meanwhile, Letty made arrangements through hospice for a hospital bed and oxygen to be delivered…not needed yet, but after they had found Angelica slipped from the armchair and crumpled onto the floor, Letty wanted to keep one step ahead.

As Angelica had lain on the floor, fully conscious but too weak to help herself, the same thoughts ran through her mind as always.

So this is suffering, this is death.

To which her soul replied: "Yes. This is death."

But why does it have to be so hard? So desperately lonely? So horrible?

"No reason, no meaning, no purpose," came the reply. "It is what it is."

This was inevitably followed by a prolonged silence until the litany of questions began over from the beginning to torment her all over again.

2

Ever since her first encounter with the bruise on her breast that had at times felt to be coalescing into a lump, other times merely a figment of her imagination, it was as if there had been two Angelicas. The two were strangers to one another, and when they met, however briefly, they argued. The first believed herself to be a realist, embracing the truth of suffering. Surrender, however, left her shivering naked before the inevitability of dying. The other Angelica, the Angelica of Angel Chi, was the one who had hope. This one dwelled upon symptoms—the phase-outs, the bitter swill—certain that mastery was but one remedy, one spiritual practice away. For this Angelica, it was just a matter of whipping a rogue cell, a random lymph node, into shape. Back and forth she ricocheted, bounced between the two Angelicas: the first of despair and the other of desperation.

The two had been with her since the onset of her illness—perhaps long before. But nevertheless, as her cancer progressed, the more the magical thoughts about such things as large quantities of oranges and the placement of crystal grids receded—and the more the inevitability of her own death advanced. Had it really been only a matter of months since she had believed that Angel Chi could save her? How inexorably, how quickly, her life had been draining away, leaving her at last crumpled on the floor, buried in the wreckage of her crushed hope.

Even now, long after having been gently raised aloft to zero gravity, yet did the loneliness of her condition weigh oppressively upon her. *In all the world, had there ever been anyone so isolated in these final lonely hours?* Turned toward the distant wailing of lighthouses, she was sandwiched between honeymooners on cruise liners holding hands at the rail before her; and the sounds of a bustling city overflowing with theater-goers, tai chi practitioners, students and strangers at her back. *Who, of all the creatures in the highest mountain village or deepest ocean floor, had ever been so utterly alone?*

3

What remained of Angelica's life now existed only as memories. Remembrances of the recent past, the last time Martin had visited, the arrival of a bouquet of the first spring flowers, sped by quickly as her thoughts drifted back again to memories from long ago, and there they stalled. The time she had walked off stage, her parents and Mira waiting for her with roses. Even earlier, drawing a picture of her first flower from life in kindergarten when, against the teacher's order, she had put a plucked red petal to her lips. The memory of the tantalizingly bitter taste of it catalyzed the very warp and weave of her childhood: her mother's cream of mushroom soup, her sister's Tiny Tears, her own prized collection of Nancy Drew mysteries.

I must control my memories or I will be unable to bear the losses, she warned herself, forcing herself back into the present. But her eyes landed upon the door jamb bearing the faded pencil marks that had charted Sophie's growth. Even the wall carried pain.

Relying on the strength of her will, she forced herself away from difficult thoughts and back to recent memories: a dish of ice cream, Sarah's gift of a leather-bound journal, only this time, her train of thought led her not to the distant past, but to reconsider the course of her illness from inception. There had been the bruise, the calcium deposits and so on and on forward to the terrifying future, and then winding back double-time to before the first cell had broken free and even earlier, before it had found a place to hide, and then to the very beginning, before it had existed at all, if there ever really were such a time. The further back her memories drifted, the greater her life force. There was a time when her optimism seemed justified, when the goodness of life was a given. But illness had called all this into question. Suffering and meaninglessness: the two were inexorably linked. *As my illness has advanced, so has my life deteriorated—and at the same pace.*

There was a time, at least one time, one thing, that had contained pure joy, she was sure of it. But now even as she made the desperate attempt to call forth a single bright memory, the shadows were lengthening, the darkness advancing. Suddenly, she was in free fall, hurtling through the void, gathering speed as she plummeted. Suffering upon suffering, the destruction of her life accelerating as she raced toward the bottom, with nothing to break her fall.

"Nothing to stop me," she cried out loud. She opened her eyes, searching for something to slow the descent, but eyes opened or closed, it was all the same. Only the horror of the final impact awaited her.

If only I could find the meaning in this, some gift, some lesson. There must be something to be learned from this, even if only I could identify where I went wrong.

But how could that be? She had always done her best, won the admiration of others, exceeded expectations.

"There is no lesson in this, not for me or for others. Death means nothing. But why?"

PART ELEVEN
The Mainland

1

It had been two weeks since the hospital bed had been installed in the downstairs living room, positioned to take advantage of the view of Casco Bay, but Angelica refused to move to it. She knew that relocating downstairs was to be the last move she would ever make, the advanced hospital equipment—with guardrails and mechanical lifts—nothing more than her death bed. But even more compelling was her desire to stay put in her study, just down the hall from Sophie's room, having, at last, cause to believe that Sophie's arrival was imminent.

The good news was that Sophie had finally received her travel documents, the bridge had been repaired, and she was ready, at last, to undertake the challenging journey through snow-covered mountainous terrain, part by foot, part by shuttle to Medog, Tibet, then by regional aircraft to the mainland: Linzhi Airport in Chengdu, China. This, in itself, would take 10 days. But then the church insisted that she follow protocol, three days layover in Chengdu to acclimate to the lower altitude.

When the time came to protest the delay, hoping to beat what had been predicted to be an earlier-than-usual start to the rainy season, she would turn out to be so dizzy and nauseous due to the sudden change of altitude upon landing there was to be no question she needed the extra time to recover. At its best, it would have then been a simple matter of making the bi-weekly flight that went direct to Incheon Airport in South Korea, from there that same day to JFK and after 15 hours in the air, the last, quick hop to Portland. As it would turn out, she would succeed in beating the rainy season, but for no explicable reason, there would also be an unlucky delay in take off from Chengdu that caused her to miss her connection, and so it was that Sophie's rush to get home turned into a race against time.

2

Late one afternoon, there was a sudden bustling downstairs. An emissary from the church was at the townhouse door with the news they'd been hoping for. Sophie had made it to the mainland. The middle-aged woman at the door, dressed in an out-of-date black suit, and oversized cross, came bearing the welcome report of progress, and a noodle casserole. Charles hurried upstairs to see if Angelica was awake and in a stable enough state of mind to take in the good news. But it was immediately apparent that over the course of the afternoon, while they thought she had been napping peacefully, Angelica had taken a sudden turn for the worse. Charles found her sitting stiffly in the recliner, staring blankly at the pencil markings that had marked Sophie's passage through childhood on the wall. Beads of sweat ran down her forehead, her jaw slack, and she was breathing rapidly. He started to shout out for Mira to call hospice. Angelica's blank eyes darted to him. And once fixed, erupted in such a blaze of rage—rage at him—he fell silent.

"For Gods' sake. Why can't you let me be," she hissed.

Just then, Mira arrived at the door, carrying a bowl of lemon jello, and Angelica turned her gaze to her with the same raw animosity.

"Is everything alright?" Mira asked, directing her concern more to Charles than Angelica.

"What do you care?" Angelica replied, in the coldest tone she could muster. "You'll be rid of me soon enough."

The two stood there in stunned silence. Mira placed the jello beside Angelica, attempting a smile, then she and Charles left together.

"Did I do something?" Charles asked Mira when they were out of range. "She's acting as if it's my fault."

"Don't worry about it Charles," Mira replied, the kindest words she'd spoken to him since she'd arrived. "Sick people are always looking for someone to blame. She doesn't mean it."

The call to hospice was made. Several hours before her regular shift was scheduled to begin, Letty arrived and immediately checked Angelica's vitals. When she felt for her pulse, Angelica pulled her arm away.

"A waste of time," Angelica muttered. "You can't fix this."

"I can help you with your pain, *Mi Tesoro*. There's no need for you to suffer."

"Ha!" Angelica replied. "As if, as if…just go. Go. All of you."

They regrouped in the living room, Charles leaning against the empty hospital bed.

"What can we do? She's too damn stubborn to take opioids," he said.

"We can start by helping her with her breathing," Letty offered, secretly sharing their frustration that Angelica would not do more for herself to ease the agony she was condemning herself to endure. The pain must be unbearable. She walked toward a canister of oxygen that had arrived with the bed order, preparing to demonstrate its usage to the family.

"But you know, it's not only about the physical pain. She is suffering—emotionally." Letty was careful to stay within bounds, offering comfort and companionship, but knowing to call in the professionals—the counselor or chaplain—when it came to ministering to moral or spiritual crisis.

Last night, 3 a.m., Angelica had bolted upright in the recliner, caught somewhere between a nightmare and delirium. Her words were garbled, but Letty could make out some of it.

"The lie, the lie" she cried, then collapsed back into the chair and shut her eyes.

But, in truth, this was neither the end, nor the beginning, of Angelica's torment. For earlier, just at the point Letty had bent down to change her socks, settling in to massage her feet, Angelica had been swept first with a wave of gratitude. *Mi Tesoro.* But even before she could relax into the gentle grasp of her genuinely caring nurse, another wave set in— this wave, lethal as a tsunami: a towering, horrifying wave of revulsion. *Only this is real. Everything else, every word, every deed, everything: what if every other moment of my life has been a lie?*

Or worse. For no, not just a lie told to her. *What if I, myself, am the lie? Imposter. Fraud.* Since falling ill, how many times had she replayed the scenes of her life, each time declaring herself innocent? Inconceivable that there had been something fundamentally wrong all along. But that was just it, the thing that had persistently taunted and evaded her, hidden in plain, horrifying sight all the while. She had been playing scenes from the first, claiming powers to which she had no right. *It was all, all of it, a lie.*

She had always played to the largest possible audience, and she always delivered what they wanted—but at what cost?

What had it cost me to be special, winning favor above the rest? Behind the counter at the pharmacy, in bed with the college director, live from The Today Show? What impulses to humility, to honesty, to true goodness had I suppressed in order to become a success? Could it possibly be that mother's disappointment in me, Master Chen's accusation of betrayal, Sophie's desertion and the odious lawsuit had been the only true things in all my life? Had that horrid woman who had brought suit been wrong about the facts, but right all along about the only thing that really mattered? What if it was true, that I, Angelica, had squandered my one opportunity to live honestly, humbly, lovingly and that everything else was lies?

Angel Chi, her marriage to Charles. Suddenly, Angelica saw clearly that nothing had been the real thing, not even her name, Angelica, was the real thing. Was it all vanity then? In the name of doing God's work, had she played the fool? Worse, played God? Thinking she had the key to beating the system, judging herself to be above the rest. She had thought it had all been out of love—wanting to save herself and others from unnecessary pain. The alternative had been unthinkable—to let helplessness and imperfection have the final say. Was it true, then? Were things actually worse for her family, her students and followers because of her, not better?

But if this were true, no chance to right the wrongs, what is left for me to do? I had one life, one opportunity to live as I should, and I squandered it.

Quieter now, convicted, she once again replayed the story of her life. But this time, she saw proof of it in real time, and it sickened her. Charles standing before her, Mira carrying in the jello, Letty's hand on her pulse: every act, every gesture, every word chiding her:

You did not live as you should have.

In Charles and Mira, she saw her dark reflection, distorted by ego, dishonesty and false pride. It had all been an illusion, looking for all the world to be masterful, powerful, but in truth, a horrific denial of life. In Letty, alone, Angelica saw the opportunity for a good life, so simple and yet so elusive, that had passed her by. This, perhaps, was the greater source of anguish. That afternoon, just before Charles entered, she opened her eyes and the agonizing truth of her ruined life failed to dissipate. Angelica broke out in a cold sweat, struggled for air. And with every word they uttered, she hated them all the more.

3

The oxygen gave Angelica an hour of much-needed relief. But by dinner time, she had ripped out the tubes and lay there moaning in the chair. Mira came to her and took her hand. "Angelica, dearest. There's something I want to ask you to do for me. It doesn't mean anything, even people in the prime of their lives—children even—say The Viddui."

"Viddui!" Angelica fought for the next breath. "Now? For me? Why?" and she moaned even louder than before. "God No!…Still…"

Her breathing quieted, and Mira, seizing the opportunity, motioned to Charles, Letty and the hospice chaplain, who had unbeknownst to Angelica been listening from the hallway. The earnest young man, non-Jewish but well-intentioned, had brought his crisp white copy of the phonetic pronunciation handout labeled "Jewish Confession for the Dying" that had been given to him during his training. He couldn't remember whether he was intended to soldier through the long, Hebrew prayer alone and was greatly relieved when Mira joined in. *"Aval anachnu chatanu,"* they began reading, first in Hebrew then in English. "Indeed, we have sinned, O my God. May it be Thy will that I sin no more, and what I have sinned wipe away in Thy mercy." The reading continued for several minutes, with one or the other stumbling over the Hebrew.

Angelica was unexpectedly moved by the prayer, tears welling up in her eyes. After, Charles and Letty adjusted the recliner into sleeping position and dimmed the lights. Mira and Letty walked the chaplain out, thanking him for a job well done. For the briefest moment, Angelica felt better than she had in weeks, suddenly daring to consider the possibility that she might live, after all, *The Phase One Trial*, she thought to herself. *Maybe it's not too late*, forgetting in her muddled state that in the end she had not qualified.

That's the real answer. I know it now— What it is I really want. I want to live—really live!

"I'm proud of you," Charles said, when the others had left, his voice shocking her back into the room. "You made your sister so happy."

"Indeed," she hissed, turning quickly away from him. And however briefly hope had touched her heart, it was gone. Charles' bloated silhouette, his pretentious black t-shirt and jeans backlit against the hallway light, the presumptuous tone in his voice—all pretense!

Pretense and lies, every bit of it. You are nothing but a fraud, a pretender…an, an actor. And everything you stand for, everything you value is a masquerade, shielding you from what's real. Life, and death: that's what's real and you, you are nothing but a great, big lie.

And with this final thought, a back draft of revulsion ignited the empty space hope had left behind and set her pain ablaze. But this pain was something new. For the first time, she felt burning licks of fire penetrating into the very marrow of her bones, and with it came the unavoidable certainty of inescapable, imminent annihilation.

Even in the dimmed light, the glare in her eyes when she'd issued the word "Indeed" was deeply unnerving to Charles. Then, with an effort he'd thought that in her weakened state would be beyond her, she shot upright and screamed:

"Stop it! Just stop it! Get out of here! Get out! Get out!"

PART TWELVE

Living Room

1

The scream that had chased Charles from the room continued for three days, interrupted only by moans and delirious words. With Martin and Flip's help, they moved Angelica downstairs to the hospital bed in the living room, attempting to make the space as welcoming as possible. Flower arrangements and plants had been arriving regularly, as word spread through their inner circle that Angelica's passing was imminent. When Angelica had refused to leave her proximity to Sophie's room, she had been mollified (only somewhat) when Charles grabbed the opened bottle of Sophie's favorite perfume from Sophie's dresser—the white jasmine she'd had to hastily leave behind—to set beside her with the bottles of medicines on the bed tray. Only Letty and Mira could remain with Angelica for more than a few minutes, Charles trembling so he dropped his bottle of beer to the floor, shattering it to pieces. Having promised Angelica no more painkillers, Letty alone held the resolve to respect her patient's rights, although it saddened her to see such unnecessary suffering.

"No! No! No!" The words fled Angelica's mouth as if trying to escape the burning within that continued unabated. "Stop it. Stop it," started as a moan but ended in a wordless scream. The moment it had begun, that moment she had shouted "Get out" to Charles, she knew all was lost. There would be no turning back.

Day turned to night and back again, but Angelica was out of time, plummeting, plummeting through nothingness, the relentless force shoving her downward through the endless pitch-black void. She resisted with all her might, but with every contortion, accelerated all the faster toward the horror that beckoned below. And in her agony, she saw the true nature of her horror, and it shocked her. For this void was not bottomless, after all. There was something there. Yes, it was a horror to be in freefall, but even more so a horror that she could not *make* herself arrive. And ironically, what was keeping her from making the free fall end was the very thing she had thought would save her: *The conviction that she had lived an exceptional life.* This belief that she could not shake had her in its grip and caused her the greatest misery of all.

Suddenly, Angelica's chest exploded, the shock of it forcing the last of the air out of her lungs and at last, she plunged to the bottom. And where there had been nothingness, Angelica found herself blinking against a brilliant beam of light shining through a crack.

Ah! Hah! All that to which I previously clung—none of it really was real. I was right. I can see this clearly now. Angelica quieted.

But what, then, is real?

2

This happened on a cold spring afternoon in Portland, the final of the three days of screaming, the last hour before her death. Martin had received Mira's call and entered the living room quietly, bearing red roses. Angelica was screaming in agony, her arms thrashing as if reaching for something. The instant Martin entered, Letty knew the scent of the roses was too heavy for the room, so briskly delegated them to the back deck, letting in a blast of salty ocean mist. Angelica's eyes flew open, her hand flailing against the tray table, sending spoons and bottles flying. She fixed a beseeching gaze on Charles, who immediately understood what she had been grasping for. He picked up the bottle of white jasmine perfume, miraculously unbroken, from the floor, and with tears streaming down his cheeks, placed it in her hand.

In that moment, Angelica Goodman Banks dropped through the crack of light and into an endless pulsating radiance, and saw that indeed her life had not been the real thing *but that it wasn't too late.* "But what is real?" she repeated, more insistently, then fell back into silence and emerging from the silence, words. *Sh'ma Yisrael. Adonai Eloheinu. Adonai Echad.* "Hear O Israel, the Lord our God, the Lord is One."

She felt someone's hands cup her own, her bony fingers still gripping the bottle of white jasmine. She felt soft, familiar lips brush her hand. Sophie? Had Sophie finally arrived home? With great effort, she raised her eyelids and beheld Charles, unbounded grief tearing her heart open. Mira now approached. Angelica regarded the stoic curve of her lips quivering with despair, and suddenly, through the cracks in her broken heart, a tidal wave of emotion engulfed her. What was this feeling she could not control? Lament. She lamented for her sister. She looked to Martin, and then she grieved for them all: for Sophie, for her mother and father, for Rena, for all those whose stories, past, present and future, were part of her own.

"This is unbearable for them," she thought. "They feel such pity, but it will pass. I know it now. God is one, God is everything, everywhere. That is the only thing that is real, so either nothing means anything—or everything does. It does not matter which I choose to believe. It will all pass when I die."

She tried to tell them, tell them that all debts had been forgiven, but the words came out garbled and they did not understand. She had to do something. She tried again, and managed the word "Forgive" but it came out "Given". Charles and Mira looked to one another, confused, but Angelica was too weak to try again.

God understands, she thought. *That's enough.* Then suddenly, she knew what it was she needed to do, for herself, for all of them. Finally, she could stop hurting them— alleviate the suffering, theirs and her own.

Of course, so obvious and so easy. And what of the pain? Has my pain dissipated as well? She searched for it, listened for it. *Oh, there you are. Well, so be it.*

And what, then, of death?

She braced herself, but death was nowhere to be found. There was only radiance. Joy! An endless field of love, infinite and eternal, overlooking nothing, embracing all.

"Perfect!" her soul marveled.

It was only a moment in real time, but the bliss was lasting. For the four who stood witness to her passing, Angelica's suffering body struggled on for an unbearably long time. At last, the bottle of white jasmine released from her grip, shattering into pieces as it hit the floor.

"She's gone," one said, when the thrashing stilled at last, the sheet covering Angelica's thin chest having risen up and then after a seemingly endless hesitation, ceased to move.

Angelica turned the words over in her soul. *So it's done. Death is done.*

The tension drained from her body and Angelica Goodman Banks sighed out her last full breath.

AUTHOR'S NOTE
For Further Study

The Death of Ivan Ilyich is considered to be one of the greatest novellas of all time, and a classic in the field of death and dying. However, outside of academic contexts, the book's cultural distance and challenged translation combine in such a way as to allow many contemporary readers to keep their emotional distance. As an expert in the field of conscious aging, I felt called to close this gap for a new generation who are grappling with the very issues of meaning and mortality Tolstoy addresses.

In the process of writing *Angelica's Last Breath*, I deconstructed *The Death of Ivan Ilyich* over the course of multiple readings, then used the framework to rebuild the story for our own cultural context and times. For individuals already familiar with Tolstoy's work, you will note that I have used some words and phrases from the original as mile markers, allowing readers of both to contrast and compare. It is my hope that readers of *Angelica's Last Breath* will be inspired to use my interpretation as a springboard into the original.

To join this conversation that both traverses and transcends the centuries, please visit the Book Club tab at CarolOrsborn.com where I have posted links to a study guide and further commentary on both *The Death of Ivan Ilyich* and *Angelica's Last Breath.* You are also invited to post comments, ask questions and dialogue with one another and the author.

ACKNOWLEDGMENTS

To contributors and readers of *Fierce with Age: The Digest of Boomer Wisdom, Inspiration and Spirituality*, and of my blog *Older, Wiser, Fiercer at CarolOrsborn.com*.

To participants in the Conscious Aging Book Club, and to Parnassus Books, Nashville.

To my co-conspirators in work and in life Robert L. Weber and Leanne Flask.

To my Nashville and Tennessee network of friends and supporters, including Emily, Jill, Judith, Pat, "Master" Elmo and my fellow tai chi practitioners, Susan Underwood, LJ Ratliff and the whole What?! Band gang.

To my mentors and friends H. Rick Moody, John Robinson, Connie Goldman, Brent Green, Rabbi Shana Mackler and The Temple community, and the good folks in-person and online who are part of Sage-ing International, SAN and the Conscious Elders Network.

To Martin O'Conner, for bringing so much chi to his photography and generously providing the cover for this book.

To the Vanderbilt Divinity School community and my fellows on the Board of Visitors.

And above all, to my family, Dan, Jody and Diego, Grant and Ginny and grandsons Mason and Dylan.

My gratitude to all of you is fierce, indeed!

BIOGRAPHY OF THE AUTHOR

Carol Orsborn is a recognized thought leader in the field of conscious aging. The most recent of her 30 books, *The Spirituality of Age: A Seeker's Guide to Growing Older*, coauthored with Harvard psychologist Robert Weber, Ph.D., won Gold in the 2015 Nautilus Book Awards in the category of Aging Consciously. Orsborn is founder and editor-in-chief of *Fierce with Age, the Digest of Boomer Wisdom, Inspiration and Spirituality*, the monthly digest dedicated to aging and spirituality. Her blog *Older, Wiser, Fierce* appears weekly at CarolOrsborn.com. She also leads The Conscious Aging Book Club at Parnassus Books in Nashville, Tennessee and online at her blog.

Dr. Orsborn received her Masters of Theological Studies and Doctorate in History and Critical Theory of Religion from Vanderbilt University with postgraduate work in Spiritual Counseling at the New Seminary in Manhattan, Stillpoint and the Spirituality Center at Mount St. Mary's College. A former top marketer helping brands like Ford, Humana and Prudential build relationships with the Boomer generation, she is now committed to both living and expanding awareness of aging as a spiritual path.

For the past forty years, Orsborn has been a compelling voice of her generation, interviewed on *Oprah*, *The Today Show*, *CBS Morning News*, *The New York Times* and *The Wall Street Journal* among many others. She speaks regularly before association and industry groups on the Boomer generation.

Dr. Orsborn lives in Nashville, Tennessee with her husband Dan, and their dogs Lucky, Molly and Sammy, a rescue from the Old Friends Senior Dog Sanctuary. She is the grandmother of two.

RELATED BOOKS BY CAROL ORSBORN

The Spirituality of Age: A Seeker's Guide to Growing Older. Coauthored with Dr. Robert L. Weber. Inner Traditions, 2015. Winner of a Gold Nautilus Award in the category of Aging Consciously. A Spanish edition of the book was released by Inner Traditions in 2018.

Fierce with Age: Chasing God and Squirrels in Brooklyn. Nashville: Turner Publishing, 2013.

The Art of Resilience: 100 Paths to Wisdom and Strength in an Uncertain World. New York: Three Rivers Press/Random House, 1997.

Nothing Left Unsaid: Words to Help You and Your Loved Ones through the Hardest Time. Berkeley, California: Conari Press, 2001.

Boom: Marketing to the Ultimate Power Consumer—the Baby Boomer Woman. With

Mary Brown. New York: Amacom Publishing, 2006.

The Silver Pearl: Our Generation's Journey to Wisdom with Dr. Jimmy Laura Smull. Chicago: Ampersand, Inc. 2005

Solved by Sunset: The Self-Guided Intuitive Decision-Making Retreat. New York: Harmony/Random House, 1996 and New York: Crown, 1997.

Speak the Language of Healing: Living with Breast Cancer without Going to War. Foreword by Jean Shinoda Bolen, M.D. With Susan Kuner et al. Berkeley, California: Conari Press, 1997.

THE INSPIRED WORKS COLLECTION

Angelica's Last Breath (Spring, 2018)

A novel inspired by Leo Tolstoy's The Death of Ivan Illyich

River Diary:
My Summer of Grace, Solitude
and 35 Geese (Summer, 2018)

A diary inspired by the writings of Thomas Merton

Older, Wiser, Fiercer:
One Woman's Meditation on the Measure
of Our Days (Fall, 2018)

Essays inspired by Florida Scott-Maxwell's The Measure of My Days

INVITATION TO STAY CONNECTED

You are invited to become a subscriber to *Fierce with Age: The Digest of Boomer Wisdom, Inspiration and Spirituality,* the free monthly publication offering excerpts of the best content about conscious aging for Boomers. Subscribe as well as gain access to the archives of past editions at *Fiercewithage.com*

For Carol Orsborn's personal blog, and for on-going conversation on the topic of spirituality and aging, visit *Older, Wiser, Fiercer* at *CarolOrsborn.com.*

Both websites also provide links to Carol's Orsborn's online presence at Facebook, Twitter and LinkedIn.

Carol Orsborn's Conscious Aging Book Club welcomes you to both in-person and online participation. The virtual club, including a reader's guide for *Angelica's Last Breath*, can be accessed at the Book Club tab on both of the above websites.

Contact Carol Orsborn at:
Carol@fiercewithage.com.

99979931R00159

Made in the USA
Columbia, SC
13 July 2018